THE TIME PATRIOT

Episode 1 - Hail Mary Pass

Kim Megahee

The Kimmer Group

Gainesville, GA

Kim Megahee/The Kimmer Group LLC
505 Rienzi Court
Gainesville, GA 30506
www.AuthorKimMegahee.com

Publisher's Note: This is a work of fiction. Names, characters, places, and incidents are a product of the author's imagination. Locales and public names are sometimes used for atmospheric purposes. Any resemblance to actual people, living or dead, or to businesses, companies, events, institutions, or locales is completely coincidental.

Book Layout © 2017 BookDesignTemplates.com

Book Title/ Author Name. -- 1st ed.
ISBN 978-1-7340190-9-4

Dedication

This book (and the rest of this series) is dedicated to my soulmate wife Martha Rice Megahee. She's the wisest person and the best judge of character I know. When she offers advice, I listen. However, technology is not her friend.

Relevant Quotes

"A lady asked Dr. Franklin Well Doctor what have we got a republic or a monarchy – A republic replied the Doctor if you can keep it." — "The Lady here alluded to was Mrs. Powel of Philada." From the Journal of James McHenry - September 18th, 1787

"Our new Constitution is now established, everything seems to promise it will be durable; but, in this world, nothing is certain except death and taxes." Benjamin Franklin - 1789

Cast of Characters

Character	Role
Astalos, Robert	The inventor/discoverer of time travel.
Astalos, Robby	Younger self of Robert Astalos.
Cutty, Ed - Lieutenant, US Army Rangers.	A member of the Ranger HERO Team.
Detweiler, Avery	President Harrison's Chief of Staff.
Drake, Michael - Retired General, US Army Rangers.	Liaison between the HERO Team and the President of the United States. Liaison between the HERO Team and the Senate Oversight Committee (chaired by Senator Lodge).
George, Trevor	Civilian member of the HERO Team. Formerly a cold case expert with the Atlanta Police Department.
Harrison, Wade	President of the United States, inaugurated in January 2037.
Hatcher, Karen "Hatch" - Captain, US Army Rangers.	Founding member of the HERO Team.
H.E.R.O.	An acronym. "Historical Event Research Organization."
Lagunas, Daisy "Daze" - Lieutenant, US Army Rangers.	A member of the Ranger HERO Team.
Lee, William "Will"	Butler, confidante, and slave of George Washington.

Character	Role
Lodge, James C.	The Elder Senator from the state of Georgia. Chairman of the HERO Team's Oversight Committee.
McKnight, Megan McAlister	Marc McKnight's wife.
McKnight, Marc - Colonel, US Army Rangers.	Operational Lead of the HERO Team. Principle Protagonist
Ritter, David	Special Agent in Charge for the Washington DC FBI office.
Sartain, Lydia	Lawyer, President of the Mount Vernon Ladies Association, the organization that preserves and protects the Mount Vernon Historical Landmark Park.
Smalls, Arthur - Lieutenant Commander, US Navy.	McKnight's Executive Officer (XO). Former Navy Seal and CIA operative. For simplicity and at his request, HERO Team members refer to him as an Army Major.
Tyler III, Winston - Major, US Army Rangers.	Reports to McKnight, who was his roommate at West Point. Mission Planner and long-term mission to gain the confidence of George Washington.
Warren, Tucker – Master Sargeant, US Army (retired)	Husband of Lydia Sartain
Washington, George	Retired General of the Continental Army. Hero of the War for Independence. Key player in the creation of the United States Constitution. Gentleman Farmer.
Wheeler, Roger "Mitch" - Captain, US Army Rangers.	Founding member of the HERO Team. Attended the Military College of Georgia at UNG in Dahlonega.

Character	Role
Wu, Kathy	Civilian member of the HERO Team. Mission planner.

The HERO Team – Army Rangers
General Mike Drake (Retired)
Colonel Marc McKnight – Team Lead (PROTAGANIST)
Major Arthur Smalls – McKnight's Executive Officer
Major Winston Tyler III – Team Lead
Captain Karen Hatcher
Captain Mitch Wheeler
Lieutenant Ed Cutty
Lieutenant Daisy Lagunas
Kathy Wu (civilian)
Trevor George (civilian)
Doctor Robert Astalos (civilian)

Spouses
Megan McAlister McKnight

FBI
SAIC David Ritter

Mount Vernon
Lydia Sartain – President of the MVLA
Master Sergeant Tucker Warren – her husband
Maya – MV employee

The Teacher
Professor Evelyn Dandridge

1937 Nazis
Reichsführer Heinrich Himmler
Colonel Hans Bittner
Karl Seekrieger (alias for Charles Murphy)

2037 Nazis
Führer Heinrich Hitzinger
Reichsführer Erik Olson (ANTAGONIST)

The Arms Dealer and Engineer
Cathair "Charles" Murphy (ANTAGONIST)

US Government
President Wade Harrison
POTUS Chief of Staff Avery Detweiler
Georgia Senator James Lodge
House Speaker Jack Pander
House Minority Leader Steve Baker
House Minority Whip Sally Rogers

Assassins
Juan Morales
Dante

Media
Mattie Porter
Bob, Mattie's boss
Greg, Maya's cousin

Big Tech
Lee Kennedy – CEO
David Osbourne – CEO

From 1787
George Washington
Will Lee
The Joyner Family

Chinese Spy
Rick

Before You Read...

If you want to get the most out of these time travel stories, watch the date and time stamps at the beginning of each scene. They are as important as any other aspect of this book.

To avoid confusion for those who haven't studied pre-World War II Germany in as much depth as history nerds like me, I have used more familiar military ranks for the 1937 and 2037 Nazi ranks and titles. Using the originals didn't add to the story; In fact, they diminished it. I pray all my brother and sister history nerds will understand and enjoy the story.

Cheers and Regards,
Kim

<u>Present Day - Thursday, February 5th, 2037 - 9:30 PM EST - The White House, Washington, DC</u>

Marc McKnight sat outside the Oval Office, waiting for the President of the United States.

He checked his watch. He'd been there for over an hour.

There's got to be something productive I can do.

He drew his phone from his pocket again and typed in another idea on how to convince an eighteenth-century man you're from the future and you need his help.

McKnight was a colonel in the Army's 75th Regiment and the leader of the HERO Team. His team used a limited time travel technology to research historical events, investigate suspicious event changes, and set history back on its original path when necessary.

When time travel capability was developed by Doctor Robert Astalos, the government classified it and appointed retired General Mike Drake to direct the operations of the HERO Team. Drake offered the operational command to McKnight and helped pick a team of Rangers and talented civilians to do the work.

HERO was an acronym. It stood for "Historical Event Research Organization." McKnight thought the name was lame, but he was a rule-follower and soldier who obeyed orders. He was a West Point grad who hailed from eastern Oregon, where he grew up in the small town of Pendleton near the Umatilla Indian Reservation. His dark hair and brown eyes came from the one-quarter of his blood that claimed Native American ancestry. He was six feet tall with skin that turned bronze in the sun. McKnight's father and his father before him served in the military as officers. He was introverted and credited his team for successful missions.

A woman approached him. He'd seen her on the TEV and recognized her as one of President Harrison's advisors, but he couldn't remember her name.

"Colonel McKnight?" she said. "The President wants you to meet with him in his private study upstairs. If you'll follow me, please?"

McKnight stood, gathered his briefcase and White House visitor badge, and followed her.

In four days, the HERO Team would begin their most important and dangerous mission ever, and he presumed the President wanted to give him a pep talk. He brought his project documentation with him in case the President wanted to discuss the plans.

McKnight was not in favor of the mission. While its goals were admirable, the risk of affecting American history was significant. In his opinion, the risks were too great for the potential rewards.

He could have declined to take part. But, he reasoned, the mission would still be executed, even if he didn't accept the command. They'd give it to someone with less experience with time travel technology. It was a hard choice, but he swallowed his objections and accepted the command.

The woman led him up a flight of stairs and down a long hallway. She stopped before a door with a brass-plated 'Private' sign and knocked.

President Wade Harrison answered the door with a cell phone to his ear, beckoned McKnight to enter, and turned away. McKnight nodded to the woman and entered the room. She closed the door behind him.

In the middle of the room, there were two small sofas facing each other across a coffee table. A table and lamp stood at each end of the sofas. On the far side of the room was a floor-to-ceiling window that offered a view of the Washington Monument.

Except for the window and door, the room dedicated every inch of wall space to bookshelves. A table with a coffee service sat against the east wall and a stepladder to reach the top shelves leaned against the west wall.

Harrison walked to the window, listening to his phone. His coat and tie were off, and his sleeves were rolled up to the elbows.

"Right," President Harrison said into his phone. "But that's your job, right? Why else would we be talking about this?"

He looked at McKnight and pointed to the sofa that faced the window.

McKnight moved to the sofa and stood beside it.

I can't sit while the President is standing.

"I don't care," Harrison said. "Coming up with a solution is your job, and then we can discuss it."

Harrison looked again at McKnight, then pointed emphatically at the sofa.

McKnight sat but stayed on the edge of the seat. If it was possible to stand at attention while sitting, he was doing it.

"Right. The monkey is still on your back. Call me back when you have solutions to discuss. Good night."

Harrison disconnected the call and turned back to McKnight.

President Wade Harrison carried himself like the Chief Executive he was. He wore his dark hair short, with a whisper of gray at his temples. He had an athletic build. His eyes were blue and constantly moved to watch every person in the room. McKnight knew those eyes missed very little.

"I'm sorry for the late meeting, Colonel. This has been a helluva day, but I wanted to talk to you before your mission begins next week."

"No problem, Mister President. Late meetings are part of the job."

"Yes, they are," Harrison said, as he sat on the opposite sofa. "At ease, Marc. Relax. There's no decorum or formality in this room. Do you have everything you need? For the mission, I mean?"

"Yes, sir, I believe so. I mean, there's always something that pops up, but the team is on board with the objective and they're the most inventive and creative people I know. I'm confident we have everything we need and can improvise if necessary."

"Good. I see you brought a briefcase. Project plans and stuff?"

"Yes, sir."

Harrison smiled. "You won't be needing them. I just wanted to talk to you in private." He rose and walked to the bookshelves on the east wall near the door.

McKnight placed his briefcase on the floor and leaned back on the sofa. It felt weird, sitting casually with the President like this. He twisted his body to the left so he could see Harrison.

"I want you to understand what's at stake here," Harrison said.

He pushed on a book, and the shelf retracted back into the wall and up, disappearing behind the shelves above. Another shelf with chrome sides slid up and forward to take its place, revealing several bottles and glasses.

"I heard you were a Jack Daniels and water guy, Marc. Is that right?"

"Yes, sir."

Harrison poured ice into two glasses and added the whiskey. He followed it with a dash of water.

"Me, too," he said. "Ever since my college days. Find something you like that's dependable and stick with it."

He handed McKnight one glass, lifted the other, and said, "Cheers."

McKnight stood, raised his glass to the President. "Cheers."

Harrison sat and directed McKnight to do the same.

"Marc, I want you to understand where I'm coming from, but I didn't want to do it in public. You have the unique experience of seeing me in a different light than anyone else."

"Yes, sir."

"Sometimes I feel like politics is all we do. I get so frustrated with all the arguments and the pushback and what do the pundits think, etcetera. It gets hard to even breathe sometimes."

"Yes, sir. It's not in my experience, but I can imagine. I'm glad this is your job and not mine… No offense intended, sir."

"Ha! None taken."

Harrison took a long sip from his drink and set the glass on the coffee table. "I'm sure you've heard it said that the government is so big it can't move fast. Members of the legislature and my administration say that all the time. But it isn't true."

McKnight raised an eyebrow. "Sir?"

Harrison chuckled. "Well, it takes time to filter through the levels of government, but the real time-killer is the politicians dragging their feet while they decide what changes will hurt them, what modifications they can profit from, and what revisions they can use to hammer the opposition. They could move a lot faster if they wanted to."

He paused, then waved it off.

"But the bottom line is they don't have incentive to solve any problem unless a huge block of the population jumps up and down. Both sides are guilty of this. If they solved a problem, what would they blame the opposition for? It's easier to beat up the opposition with the same old problems than to work at finding new ones."

"Yes, sir."

"But I guess it's always been that way. Ever wonder why Presidents come into office all excited and vigorous, then leave with much more gray hair and lines on their faces? In my opinion, it's the constant pounding of politics from every direction."

Harrison picked up his glass and sipped. Then he shrugged.

"But I'm getting off topic here. I didn't invite you here to complain about politics. I have more important things to say."

He set the glass back on the coffee table.

"It's no secret to anyone that our government is off track. Wanda Taylor and I have talked about this for years."

McKnight nodded. Former President Taylor endorsed Harrison for President and Harrison had been a frequent guest at her White House. They were more than friendly politicians and allies. They were friends.

"The American people are suspicious of their government. After two hotly contested elections and rumors of cheating on both sides, it's no wonder they don't trust us. Every time you turn around, there are reports of politicians taking money for favors and providing cover for people who should be in jail. Again, on *both* sides of the aisle."

"Yes, sir."

I can't argue with that.

"And now there's a genuine threat of civil war bubbling up in the Midwest. There's nothing I can say to relieve the situation because there's no excuse for all this… crap. They're upset and frustrated, and demanding change and I can't reason them out of it because, hell, I *agree* with them. They're *right*."

McKnight could sense the President's anger rising.

Be careful what you say. Presidents make big mistakes when they get pissed off.

Harrison seemed to sense his thoughts. He smiled, and said, "Don't worry, Marc. I won't drag you into the politics around this. Your focus is on the mission, and that's how it should be.

"When I became President, I made a conscious decision to move to the center. I want to be a President for all the people. The people get it, but it outrages both parties in Congress."

He chuckled. "My party calls me a traitor, and the other party suspects my actions. Both are threatening to start an impeachment movement and they could get it done with some strategic horse trading across parties. They're convinced they'd do better with my Vice President."

He drained his glass.

"So, I have one good shot at this. The idea is simple — I want to put the one man who has any chance of credibility with the American people in front of them to share what he and the other Founding Fathers were trying to do with the American Constitution. We have the technology to do this, but I agree it's risky."

McKnight nodded. "Yes, sir."

Harrison leaned forward and looked McKnight in the eye.

"General Drake tells me you don't approve of the mission. I think I understand why, but I want to hear it from you. Why do you object to it, Marc?"

"Yes, sir." McKnight paused to gather his thoughts. Then he slapped his thighs with both hands and moved forward on the sofa to match the President's posture. "Sir, I'm okay with the goal of the mission. People would listen to what he has to say. But the chances of success are low, and the risks are off the scale. What if something happens to him and he doesn't make it back to the Constitutional Convention? What if he visits our time and is so discouraged by what he finds, he chooses not to take part in politics anymore? For God's sake, what if someone *shoots* him?"

McKnight paused.

Is he with me?

Harrison said nothing.

"Sir, if any of that occurs, America as we know it would never exist. Everything we've built here... the freedoms, the industries, the food production, the military might... Everything would change. Sure, some good ideas would catch on, but the best scenario — continuing with the Articles of Confederation and trying to tweak them — would leave us a bunch of squabbling states. Just like Europe was in the same time period."

"Yes," Harrison said, "I see that risk. And what else?"

McKnight blinked.

Isn't that enough?

"Okay, sir. Let's just look at where the man himself is, along with the technology limitations. We can only travel to years that are a multiple of twenty-five years from the current time. Because of the travel limitations, now is the best time to go. From now, in February 2037 to February 1787. That's two months before the Constitutional Convention. And it's two years before he takes office, and ten years before he has the experience of leaving the office."

"Yes, and we can't afford to wait. Please go on."

He wants me to get all my objections on the table. Okay, here goes.

"Yes, sir, and we haven't considered what to do if he comes back with us and doesn't want to cooperate, or if he flat out refuses to come to 2037. How do you convince an eighteenth-century man, even a forward-thinking one like Washington, that you came from 250 years in the future, but you need his help? I mean, we have a planned approach, but what if he doesn't buy it? Sir, all these outcomes point to dismal failure."

"What's your bottom line, Marc?"

"We're much more likely to fail than succeed... Sorry, sir."

His glass in hand, the President stood, and McKnight stood as well.

Harrison shook his head and said, "No, don't stand. Sit. Relax. I'm just letting your words sink in."

McKnight lowered himself back onto the sofa.

"I think we agree, Marc," Harrison said. "The mission is a Hail Mary pass. We're down four points in the fourth quarter with three seconds left on the clock. All the things you brought up are risks we cannot control or mitigate. Would you like another drink?"

"No, sir, I'm fine."

Harrison set his glass back on the bottle shelf and returned to his sofa.

"So, here's where we are, Marc. If we go into civil war, we lose power and we embolden our enemies. Who'd move in first? China? Russia? North Korea? India? All the above? At minimum, they'd make territorial conquests elsewhere in the world that we'd never permit if we were stronger."

He paused, and McKnight nodded.

He's right.

"Can you imagine this world without freedom?" Harrison said. "We can't afford a civil war. The *world* can't afford it. For 250 years, the United States has been a beacon of freedom and opportunity in the world. That's why people are trying to get into our country and not out of it. If the United States fails, the world descends into darkness. The United States has been the greatest experiment in government of all time and, until recently, has been overwhelmingly successful. And now? We haven't failed, but we've stumbled badly. If we don't get back up and past this, we'll slide further from freedom, with more fighting in the streets and more deaths of innocents. What happens next depends on whether we Americans can find our vision again."

"Yes, sir."

"Marc, you've seen me as President, but you and your team also found me on another timeline as a poor public servant, struggling to make a difference."

"Yes, sir."

He means where we found him before we set history back on its original track.

"You see, Marc? I have to try. I can't stand by and watch us go down if I can prevent it. I will not shy away from action — it's my duty as President. Does that make sense to you?"

"Yes, sir."

"From my point of view, the biggest driver behind all the fighting and insurrection is politics. Do you agree?"

"You could make that case, sir. People follow their favorite politicians, sometimes without question."

"Right. And the politicians of both parties keep their gravy train going by staying in power, so they take every opportunity to whip up angry emotions against the opposition and portray themselves as

benevolent saviors. And the media falls right in with them —
sensationalizing every event on the nightly news. We need to turn it
around."

"Sir?"

"I mean to shine a bright light on the process. Expose the
politician's racket to everyday Americans — the hardworking people
who are too busy making a living to educate themselves on the issues
—"

"The politician's racket, sir?"

"Yes, you know what I mean — the system where a person can
make a career of 'public service' and get wealthy. That's what I want
the American people to see. If they ever understand it, they'll insist we
fix it. America needs citizen legislators, not career politicians. We
want people in Congress who are motivated by the problems they can
solve, not the wealth they can generate."

McKnight nodded.

*Unless I'm reading him totally wrong, he's serious. He wants to
make things better.*

"If anyone can explain where the Founders were coming from, it
would be Washington, wouldn't it?" Harrison said. "We have to try,
and I need you to be on board with that. But we can't manipulate him
to our side. We need to hear from the real guy — the one who put his
life on the line during the fight for independence and dragged us,
kicking and screaming, into a democratic republic. Can you support
that, Marc? Are you with me?"

"Yes, sir. I can do that."

As he left the White House and drove home, McKnight replayed
their discussion in his head.

*A masterful performance? Maybe. But he's right. It's a Hail Mary
pass and we have to go for it.*

CHAPTER TWO

<u>Nineteen months earlier - Friday, July 27, 2035 - 10:06 PM EST - A park in Suburban Washington DC</u>

Cathair "Charles" Murphy scanned the park around him for anything suspicious. He sat on a bench, ran a freckled hand through his red hair, and pulled out his phone.

The transaction he completed earlier today might allow him to retire in style if he chose to.

If I can find the right person to buy it.

He searched his directory of clients until he found the one he wanted and pressed the call button.

A sleepy voice answered.

"Hallo?"

"Hello," Murphy said. "This is Cathair Murphy with a message for Herr Hitzinger."

The voice on the other end of the line switched from German to English. "Thank you for calling, Herr Murphy. What is the message?"

This has to be said in just the right way.

"Are you recording this?"

"Yes, mein Herr."

"Good. Please tell Herr Hitzinger that Cathair Murphy called. I have two items for sale that I'm certain he'll be interested in. One of them is information. The other is a set of technology blueprints. Once he reviews the two, he will understand that the technology is far more important than the information, but the two together could change the world most agreeably. That's the message. Do you have it all?"

"Ja, I do, Herr Murphy. If Herr Hitzinger is interested, when can he call you and at what number?"

Murphy chuckled. "He has my number, sir, and he knows he can call me anytime. Do you have questions?"

"No, sir. Is there anything else?"

"No. Auf Wiedersehen."

Murphy disconnected the call.

We've watched America support the British again and again at the expense of us Irish. But the winds of changes are in the air.

****

Present Day - Friday, February 6th, 2037 - 08:22 PM EST - The Oval Office

Retired General Mike Drake sat on the sofa in the Oval Office. His thinning blonde hair was turning gray. He stood five foot ten, with a Greek nose and steely gray eyes. And he wished he was elsewhere.

I hope Lodge hasn't killed our mission.

Senator James Lodge sat next to him on the couch. The Senator was a towering figure, standing at six-five and carrying 250 pounds. He wore a full head of light brown hair and brown eyes.

They stood when the President of the United States entered the office.

This won't be fun.

"Good afternoon, gentlemen," President Harrison said. "Thanks for coming by and please be seated." He sat on the sofa across from them. "Did you get coffee or whatever? Do you need anything?"

"We're fine, sir," Drake answered, and Lodge nodded. "May we join everyone else in congratulating you on your inauguration?"

"Thanks, Mike. It's great to be here, but now the actual work starts."

"Yes, sir. We'll be happy to help in any way we can," Lodge added.

"Good." Harrison said, as he turned to him. "Jim, you sounded concerned when you called. Do I need to be worried about tomorrow's mission?"

Lodge shifted in his chair. "I don't think so, sir, but I thought we should discuss it. It could be nothing."

"But you were concerned enough to call me?"

Drake glanced at Lodge.

I'm glad I'm not him.

"Well, I discussed it with Mike, and we decided it was worth a quick meeting with you."

Wonderful. Drag me into your mess. Thanks.

"Yes, Mr. President," Drake said. "But it could be nothing."

"Okay. So lay it out for me. What's the deal?"

Lodge met Drake's eyes, then turned back to the President.

"It seemed innocent enough at first, sir, but here are the details. Yesterday, I met with a Mister Charles Murphy. A woman who identified herself as a special assistant to Henry Lord made the appointment. Henry Lord is the CEO of MBZ Corporation. He's also a friend, a constituent, and a major donor. So Elizabeth fast-tracked the appointment."

"And?"

"When Murphy showed up, he invited me at length to speak at the grand opening of MBZ's expansion in Ireland next year. He threw out a bunch of details and sounded like the Wikipedia file on MBZ."

"Sounds normal," the President said.

"Yes, sir, it does. Except he left a bug under the edge of my desk."

"He did? Why did you check? I mean, what made you suspect he wasn't on the level?"

"I don't know, sir. It just didn't feel right. I've been in office a long time and get asked to attend events all the time. This invite just seemed... too perfect. So I asked Elizabeth to call Henry, and she learned he doesn't know Murphy."

"I see."

"Yes, sir. So I checked the edge of the desk and found the bug. I passed it on to security for examination. Elizabeth ran down to the street with them to see if Murphy was still in the area, but he was gone."

"So that was the end of it?"

Lodge fidgeted in his chair. "No, sir. Mike and I chatted on the phone while Security was checking for fingerprints. We discussed the mission."

Bad mistake. He shouldn't have called me from that room until security cleared it.

"After fingerprints, they did an electronic scan. There was a second bug on the back of the chair Murphy sat in. Security advises the bug was powerful enough to pick up my side of the conversation, and maybe more."

The President frowned. "Did you discuss anything that might jeopardize the mission if the information fell into the wrong hands?"

"No, sir."

The President looked at Drake.

"No, sir," Drake replied. "We discussed where we were going and why, but that's about it."

"Mike, is there any reason to worry about the impact on the mission? Could this guy foul things up?"

"No, sir," Drake said. "Not unless he has a time machine. The Russians and the Chinese are working on it, but they haven't succeeded yet, as far as I know. Do you have any updates on that subject that I haven't heard about, sir?"

The President shook his head. "No, I haven't. If I remember correctly, the Army took control of the technology. The Senate Technology Oversight committee has a copy of the blueprints under lock and key. Right, Jim?"

Drake looked at Lodge. The man didn't move or blink.

What?

He looked back at Harrison, whose face was like stone.

What do they know that I don't?

Harrison waved his hand at Lodge. He didn't expect an answer to his question.

He looked back and forth between the two men. "Do either of you suspect someone else has access to the technology?"

"No, sir," Lodge said.

Drake shook his head. "Mr. President, I'd never say never, especially since we've encountered folks from the future who have the technology. But... I don't have any reason to believe anyone else has it in this time space."

"Okay." President Harrison leaned back for a moment. "Then the mission is still on. Is there anything else?"

"No, sir," they said, and rose along with Harrison when he stood.

"Thanks for the report," he said. "Now, if you'll excuse me, Homeland Security is waiting to give me an update on the Mississippi confrontation."

"Is it getting worse, sir?" Drake asked.

Harrison paused and looked at Drake.

"Worse than being on the brink of civil war?" he asked, then smiled weakly. "We're at a standoff that could go either way. That's not classified."

"Good luck, sir." Drake said. Lodge followed him out of the Oval Office.

Drake noticed Lodge was moving slower than usual. He seemed tentative with his steps.

"Jim, are you okay?"

Lodge smiled at Drake, then grimaced.

"Yeah, I'm fine," he said. "I've been having a little stomach issue. I'm seeing the GI doctor the day after tomorrow. Probably nothing. Just getting old, I guess. Every week, something else hurts or isn't working right."

You don't look fine to me.

"Okay, Jim. Well, I hope you feel better. I'll see you next week."

"Sure thing," Lodge said. "Oh, for the mission kickoff, why don't you cover the 'what' with the team and I'll cover the 'why'. Sound like a plan?"

"Yes, that's fine. See you Monday."

Lodge turned and trudged down the corridor. Drake watched him until he disappeared around a corner, then shook his head.

That guy is in a lot of pain.

CHAPTER THREE

Monday, February 9th, 2037 - 8:50 AM EST - Telegraph Road
Conference Room, Alexandria, Virginia

McKnight sat in the large conference room and sipped coffee. In
ten minutes, he would lead the mission kickoff briefing... the mission
they planned and trained for during the last six months.

Major Arthur Smalls entered the conference room and paused.

"I thought I'd be the first one to the meeting for a change."

McKnight smiled and nodded at his new executive officer.

"The coffee's ready and in the back," he said.

Smalls stood five foot ten. With his groomed mustache and his
impeccable style in clothes, most people took Smalls for a high-dollar
accountant at first glance. His major in school was indeed accounting,
but he enlisted in the Navy right out of college and joined the SEALs.
Later in his career, he left the Navy to work for the CIA. He joined the
HERO Team in the previous mission, during which his fighting ability
and strategic sense proved his value. When the HERO Team doubled
in size and Tyler got his own team, Smalls asked to join McKnight's
team as his executive officer.

Smalls walked to the coffee service as Major Winston Tyler, and
Lieutenants Daisy Lagunas and Ed Cutty entered the room.

"Good morning, Colonel," Tyler said as they passed on the way to
coffee.

McKnight raised his cup to the trio.

Tyler and McKnight were roommates at West Point. When
McKnight assumed command of the HERO Team, Tyler was his first
recruit. Unlike McKnight, Tyler had wavy blonde hair and an

outgoing personality. He served as a mission planner, a mission leader and, until recently, McKnight's executive officer.

Cutty and Lagunas also joined the HERO Team during the previous mission. They reported to Tyler.

Daisy Lagunas was a Hispanic woman from El Paso. She stood five foot six and brought street-savvy to the Team. She excelled in pistol marksmanship. Lagunas preferred to be called 'Daze' instead of 'Daisy' — she considered her first name an obstacle to gaining respect in a fighting unit.

Ed Cutty was a large man with sandy hair and brown eyes. At six-two, he weighed in at 220 pounds and could carry his weight in munitions if the mission required it. An accomplished sniper, he preferred to use the big caliber weapons in a firefight.

Doctor Robert Astalos followed them through the door. The inventor of the time engine, he spent most of his time improving the engine and peripheral equipment to enhance its usefulness. Astalos hailed from Atlanta, and his actual age was 107 years. He lived through the years 2000 to 2025 three times during the engine's development. He was extremely cognitive and agile for his age. In his spare time, he taught advanced physics classes to Hatcher and Wheeler, and taught Kathy Wu and Trevor George to run the time engine.

Astalos sat next to McKnight, with his notepad and pen on the table.

When Captains Wheeler and Hatcher entered the room, along with Doctor Kathy Wu and Trevor George, McKnight looked at his watch.

My people are here. Where's the General and Senator Lodge?

He stood. "They should be here by now. I'll go meet them at Security."

****

Monday, February 9th, 2037 - 9:01 AM EST - Telegraph Road Conference Room, Alexandria, Virginia

There they are.

Senator Lodge and General Drake entered the Historical Event Research Organization Headquarters. McKnight felt honored to work with Drake. During his active duty, Drake earned a reputation as a fierce warfighter. Even in retirement, the people who served with him referred to him as the Dragon.

After the two men cleared security, he approached them and saluted Drake.

"General Drake, Senator Lodge, it's great to see you both."

Lodge nodded and smiled.

"General Drake, are we good? The mission, I mean?" McKnight said.

"Yes, we are, Marc. The President gave the go-ahead."

Great!

"Congratulations to you and Megan on your marriage, Colonel," Lodge said. "I understand you honeymooned in the Rockies? Estes Park, if I remember correctly?"

McKnight smiled. "Yes, it was, Senator. Thank you for remembering."

"Yes," Drake said. "How was it? Did you guys see some sights?"

"Yes, sir, we did. Rocky Mountain National Park was on both our bucket lists. Estes Park is a beautiful place."

"I have no doubt," Lodge said. "Well, let's get to the briefing."

McKnight nodded. "Yes, sir. Follow me, please."

He escorted them to the conference room. Lodge and Drake sat across from Astalos near the head of the table, leaving it for McKnight as the head of the HERO Team and the mission leader.

"Good morning, ladies and gentlemen," McKnight said. He gestured toward Drake and Lodge. "And of course, our honored guests... welcome to the pre-mission briefing for what may be the most important mission we've ever undertaken. Before we start, I think General Drake and Senator Lodge have some brief remarks. General, sir?"

Drake stood and went to the lectern.

"I have little to say," he said. "You all know me and how I feel about influencing history. On this mission, we'll run a risk of doing just that. But I believe the purpose of the mission is worth the risk. The thrust is to bring George Washington from 1787 to the present to talk to the American people. We hope he'll remind them what the Founding Fathers were thinking about when they forged this government. We want him to clear up any misunderstanding about what they expected the government to do."

Drake let his words sink in.

"That's the What of the mission. I'll turn the lectern over to Senator Lodge to explain the Why. Senator?"

Lodge rose and carried his six-foot-four frame to the lectern.

"Thanks, Mike. I appreciate that description of the What. So, here's the Why."

Lodge looked around the room.

"Tomorrow, you'll be embarking to do your nation a great service. The country is in trouble. Political parties have divided our people, and now we're on the verge of another civil war. War could become real with just a spark in the wrong place. Many think we have strayed from our Founding Fathers' intentions. Our Supreme Court, which is supposed to judge the constitutionality of laws, is interpreting laws by personal politics instead. Separation of powers was supposed to keep the three branches from abusing their power. Over time, it's disintegrated and people of each branch are colluding to govern for their own benefit, not for the people's benefit.

"This mission is a shot in the dark. Some call it a Hail Mary pass at the end of a losing game, and they could be right. But we'd be remiss if we didn't use all the tools at our disposal to fix things, or at least make them better. I know this team will make it happen if it can be done. Remember, our nation depends on you."

Lodge scanned the room again, making eye contact with each person. "That's the charge for you. I wish each of you all the luck Heaven can spare you."

There was no sound in the room except breathing and the central air system.

Lodge motioned for McKnight to approach the lectern. He shook his hand, then said to the room, "I have to leave now for a meeting in the Senate, but I wanted to explain what's at stake. Good luck."

The men and women around the table stood as he waved goodbye and left the room. General Drake followed him through the door.

"This is different from our usual missions," McKnight said.

"Well, that's an understatement," Tyler said.

McKnight almost smiled but forbade his face to show it.

"We'll start the briefing in a moment, when General Drake returns. Help yourself to coffee, tea, or soft drinks in the back of the room."

The team refreshed their drinks and returned to their seats. After five minutes, Drake returned, and McKnight called the briefing to order.

"Okay, let's get started," he said. "By the way, Major Tyler laid out the mission plan, but recently, he availed himself of help from Doctor Wu, Doctor Astalos, and Major Smalls. The four of them have worked hard to cover as many contingencies as possible.

"Now, here's the opportunity. History tells us that, after the War for Independence and before becoming the first President, Washington went back to being a gentleman farmer at Mount Vernon. One of the business opportunities he recognized was that it would be profitable if he found a trade route from the Cumberland area down to the east coast via the Potomac River. He also owned some land in the west that was given to him by the British for his service in the French and Indian War. In pursuit of the trade route and to check on his properties, he made several trips from Mount Vernon back up the Potomac River. He wanted to ensure his tenants cared for his land, and he wanted to find out if the Potomac River levels would support the level of commerce needed for the venture to be successful.

"As it turns out, the project was too difficult to be profitable. But he spent a lot of time in these mountains and that's our opportunity to meet him in private and avoid as much history influence as possible. He made these trips alone or in small parties. Sometimes he and his personal valet, William Lee, made the trip alone.

"Once we find him, we'll try to explain who we are and why we've come, then convince him to return with us to the present for a couple of weeks. According to history, he was usually out in the wilderness longer than that. We'll share the original Constitution and Bill of Rights with him as proof of who we are. We want him to see his signature on the Constitution. That's the bait, because at the current time in 1787, he's already in contact with others about the inadequacies of the Articles of Confederation... people like Alexander Hamilton, John Jay, and James Madison. The text of the Constitution is the sum total of all the compromises they'll make at the Constitutional Convention. He'll no doubt be interested.

"On the other hand, he might not be inclined to trust us at all. We're hoping our weaponry and other technology will prove to him we're telling the truth. By all accounts, he's astute and cagey. He'll question every thing we say and do.

"If he comes back with us, we'll isolate him for a couple of days so he can get acclimated and study the Amendments after the Bill of Rights. After that, we're hoping to have him speak to the American people about what the Founding Fathers intended. If he wants to, he can meet with anyone in the government and ask questions. It's important to note that we shouldn't try to influence him. President Harrison wants us to help him explore the facts of how today's government functions."

"So far, I've talked about the reasons for the mission. Are there questions?"

"Yes, sir," Smalls said. "We're catching General Washington before any of the real horse-trading or negotiations about the Constitution takes place. Our access to that era is constrained by the twenty-five-year limitation. But wouldn't it be better to wait and catch him later this year?"

"Good question, Major," McKnight said. He leaned on the lectern and tried to relax. "My preference would be to talk to Washington after his terms as President," McKnight said, "but we don't have that option. As far as later this year goes, President Harrison tells us he doesn't think we can wait. He believes we're sitting on a powder keg, just waiting for a spark that'll blow it up. Once that happens, all bets are off. There's no telling what will happen. The contention between the political parties continues to push them further apart, and it's happening as some predicted, except now it's moving much faster than expected. A blowup is imminent, he says, and we need to provide a way to release some of the pressure."

McKnight glanced around the room. "Any more questions on this part?... No?... Okay, let's move on. Major Tyler's team is the advance party. They will locate General Washington in the wilds of the mountains of Northern Virginia.

"Sometime between late January and early February of 1787, he'll make his last trip alongside the Potomac to the Cumberland region. Major Tyler's team will go in tonight at 8:00 PM and go to his last known location and track him from there. Lieutenant Cutty has been shadowing Mount Vernon for the last few weeks and saw Washington leave the plantation for the west. As of yesterday, he was still trailing him. He's now where, Lieutenant Lagunas?"

"Yes, sir. Cutty sent us a status message about an hour ago. He pinpointed General Washington's location at about fifteen miles southeast of Harper's Ferry. He's accompanied by one person, his valet William Lee. By tonight, he should be close to Harper's Ferry. We'll jump in close to there tonight, catch up to Cutty, and recon where General Washington spends the night and be ready to make contact in the morning."

"Very good, Lieutenant," McKnight said. "Then my team — me, Major Smalls, Hatcher, and Wheeler — will jump in tomorrow to a location specified by the advance team. Then we'll all converge on the General and make contact."

"Sir, a question?" Kathy said.

General Drake recruited Kathy Wu as the main mission planner and the first civilian on the team. She was Asian, wore a ponytail, and stood five foot four. Kathy had research skills from her degrees in psychology, economics, and political science. She possessed an eidetic memory, allowing her to remember everything she read or saw. Except on formal occasions, she disliked being called Doctor Wu, and she loved to quote movie dialog as a tension reliever. She also was politically incorrect at every opportunity.

"Sure, Kathy. Go ahead."

"Well…" she said, "What if he doesn't want to come with you? Back to the present, I mean. What do we do?"

"Excellent question, Kathy. We'll have to cross that bridge when we come to it. We'll have our technology and the documents to show him, and we'll have to hope he will go along. On the other hand, he might not buy our story at all. A demonstration of time travel might be required. But he realizes the Articles of Confederation are not working well enough. He's shrewd enough to want to stack the deck where he can. We'll see."

"Yes, sir," Kathy said. "Me, I'm worried that he will sense our urgency, but not understand our motivation. Or he might be ready to retire, and it'll take one of the other Founding Fathers to get him to move. That's the way I read the history."

"And you might be right. Next question? Hatcher?"

"Yes, sir. No one's mentioned the impact if General Washington takes back what he learns here and uses it to influence the Convention in 1787. Aren't we concerned about that?"

"I'll take that question," Drake said, and stood. "There is a mitigation strategy in place, and I'm confident it will avoid that contingency. We've got that handled. Any more questions about that?"

"No, sir," Hatcher said. Her face was like stone.

Hatcher doesn't buy it. He didn't answer the question to her satisfaction.

"Okay, if there are no other questions…?" McKnight asked. "Good. The advance team will meet here tonight at 7:30 PM to jump out at 8:00 PM. The rest of us will meet here tomorrow morning at 7:30 AM for a jump at 8:00 AM. Dismissed."

As the members of the HERO Team filed out of the conference room, Drake pulled McKnight aside.

"I wish I was going with you," he said.

"Yes, sir. But if he comes back with us, you'll meet him soon enough."

Drake nodded. "Let me share some thoughts with you."

"Yes, sir."

Drake sat, and McKnight followed suit.

"First and foremost," Drake said, "Washington saw himself as an aristocrat — part of the upper end of society. Remember, the richest homes in New York hosted him at parties whenever they could get him to attend."

"Yes, sir?"

"I'm saying the way you communicate with him is important. Much of his dialog will be more formal than we're used to. Our normal way of speaking may strike him as uneducated or too familiar. I believe you need to establish your posture with him as an equal except in rank. So mimic his speech as much as possible. Be formal and accommodating. Pay him the full respect he deserves. In the previous ten years, he went through hell. Give him credit for that. He'll see you as an equal and will be more likely to listen to your proposal. Make sense?"

"Yes, sir, it does."

"Good. Next point. Don't go too fast with Washington. He's shrewd, but we're 250 years ahead in experience, history, and technology. Remember that, to his eyes, any technology advanced enough to defy explanation is indistinguishable from magic. He might have trouble seeing your gear and weapons as technology, and he's a religious man, so anything that appears like magic... well, it'll cross his mind that the technology might be something evil. Take your time and watch his responses. Keep this in mind, because if you lose him on that stuff, he won't come with you."

"Yes, sir," McKnight said.

"And one more thing. In the war, he experienced a lot of treachery, so he'll be cautious. His natural response to someone he doesn't know will be skepticism. I would advise that you keep nothing from him. He's a retired general and smart enough to understand nuance. Got it?"

"Yes, sir."

Drake rose from his chair. "I need to be going. Good luck, Marc. And bring me back a general."

"We'll do our best, sir."

Ask him now.

"Sir, about Hatcher's question..."

Drake smiled. "Don't worry, Marc. We've made some strides in hypnotherapy. We'll be able to manage the risk. Just keep focused on the job at hand and we'll solve the other problems if Washington comes back with you."

Damn. Now, I'm skeptical.

Drake shook McKnight's hand, then turned and walked away toward the building's entrance.

This is going to be hard.

McKnight went back to his office and tried to do some unrelated paperwork, but he couldn't concentrate. He found himself growing less worried and more excited.

If all goes well, tomorrow I'll be talking to the first President of our country.

CHAPTER FOUR

Tuesday, February 10th, 2037 - 2:13 AM EST - Home of Colonel
Marc McKnight, Alexandria, Virginia

McKnight awoke with a start. His wife Megan leaned over him.

"What? What's wrong?" he said.

"I should ask you. You were having a nightmare."

"I—I was?"

"Yes, you started thrashing around. I got up to avoid getting
smacked."

McKnight yawned and got up on one elbow. "Sorry, babe. I—
Well, I'm sorry."

"Do you remember the dream?"

He was still half asleep. He tried to focus on the dream.

"I don't."

"No? From the way you were moving, it seemed like it was pretty
vivid."

He laid back and stared at the ceiling. He could almost see it. The
dream was right at the edge of his memory.

She walked around to her side of the bed and slipped between the
sheets. She crawled over next to him, propped up on her elbow, and
laid her hand on his bare chest.

"Was it that same dream you keep having?" Megan said. "The one
about the hallway?"

Her words triggered his memory. The dream slipped from his
subconscious into vivid detail.

"Ah, yes, the same one."

He tried to relax and go back to sleep, but the dream details
sharpened. Like every time before — the minor details, the dialog, the

lights — they varied from dream to dream. But the main aspects never changed.

He was captured during a mission. He escaped into a dark hallway with a pair of dim overhanging lights. Complete escape was beyond a door at the end of the hallway. If he stood still, nothing happened. But if he moved down the hall to escape, men appeared out of nowhere and constrained his arms. The man in dark clothes and a fedora appeared, his face obscured by shadow. He held an ancient Webley pistol and spoke with a British accent. He pulled the time beacon from McKnight's neck and said something about "no inexplicable disappearances". Then the men dragged him back through a door, away from escape.

"I see a pattern," she said.

He opened his eyes and looked at her. "You do?"

She nodded. "I do. Wanna know what my theory is?"

McKnight raised up on his elbow. "Yeah, what's your theory?"

"You always have that dream right before an important mission."

"Always?"

"Well, almost always. I think sometimes you have that nightmare, but don't tell me."

Uh-oh. Busted.

"Maybe," he said. "I haven't noticed that."

Well, I haven't, really.

"Liar," she said, and kissed him on the cheek. "I know you don't want me to worry. But there's more to my theory."

"Okay."

"There are two things at play here…"

"I'm listening."

"One thing is that you hate to lose and you're pretty obsessive with your planning. You're terrified of making a mistake."

"I *do* hate to lose. But I'm not afraid of screwing up. I just don't want to let my team down."

"Okay," she said. "Say what you will, mister, but I've got your number."

You might be right.

He yawned and shrugged. "Okay, what else? What's the other thing?"

She blinked and laid back on her pillow.

"You'll think this is stupid. I'm not sure the idea makes any sense anyway."

"Try me."

She turned her head toward him and searched his face for a few seconds.

"Okay," she said. "Here goes."

She sat up in the bed and wrapped the covers around herself.

"Some people believe dreams foretell actual events. They're premonitions of something that will happen to you."

McKnight laughed.

"Don't make fun of me. Marc, they transported your body across time. What if increased perception is a side effect of time travel? Could it be that time travel enhances your consciousness? Have you ever thought of that? What if the travel makes you smarter or gives you access to more of your brain?"

"Are you kidding? Half the time I feel dumber from the travel."

"That's not funny."

"Yes, but it's just as possible as what you said." He sat up and faced her. "This feels like voodoo science or a great idea for a science fiction novel."

He regretted it as soon as it came out of his mouth.

"Hmmpf! Forget I said anything."

She laid down and turned her back to him.

"Honey… I'm not…"

Nothing I can say will help. I blew it.

He touched her shoulder and said, "I'm sorry."

She didn't respond.

McKnight laid on his back and tried to go back to sleep, but sleep wouldn't come.

He replayed the dream in his head.

I guess it could be stress.

He recalled an experience from his first mission, a cold case murder investigation in 1984. Enormous energy radiated from a young woman near where he was hiding. Though she was unaware of his presence, he experienced an almost irresistible urge to reveal himself to her and share that moment.

That wasn't normal, but it was real. What if she's right?

He closed his eyes and chastised himself.

I have enough worries without getting wrapped around the axle with some wild theory.

But the idea refused to go away.

Maybe I'll run it by Doctor Astalos and Kathy...

****

Tuesday, February 10th, 2037 - 7:30 AM EST - HERO Team Lab, Telegraph Road, Alexandria, Virginia

McKnight yawned as he walked from his office to the Lab.

Not enough sleep last night. Call it excited, nervous, stressed, apprehensive? Whatever.

All those emotions applied. He woke up too early this morning, so he did what he always did when he couldn't go back to sleep — He got up, showered, got dressed, and went to work. He had been here since 6:00 AM.

When he arrived at the office, he stopped off in the locker room and slipped on the buckskin shirt of his period costume. Then he stopped.

We should look different if we want to convince Washington we come from somewhere else.

He pulled the shirt off, put his combat uniform back on, and went to his office to do some paperwork.

He heard movement down the hall and glanced at his watch.

Time for the others to arrive.

He went to greet them in the Lab.

As usual, Hatcher and Wheeler were already there. Smalls entered the Lab at the same time as McKnight.

His three reports came to attention and saluted.

Wheeler and Hatcher were sitting at the break room table in the Lab. They were charter members of the HERO Team. They had been best friends and teammates since their underclassmen days at the Ranger School at the University of North Georgia. Late last year, both were promoted to captain and assigned to Smalls.

Despite his name, Mitch Wheeler was Hispanic. He grew up in the mean streets of Detroit. An extrovert, Wheeler never met a stranger. He was an expert in physics, planning, and was strong for his five-foot-nine frame. Wheeler loved to tell outlandish stories to his comrades and friends. He worked out hard at the gym every day.

Karen Hatcher grew up in North Georgia. She was an introvert who disliked small talk. She was tall and always wore her jet-black hair in a ponytail. Hatcher looked like the girl next door with freckles on her face. Graceful as a dancer, she was also lethal in hand-to-hand combat. Most days, you could find her honing her fighting skills at the gym. Though many tried, no one had ever defeated her in a fighting match except McKnight, who only did it once.

The first thing Wheeler and Hatcher had in common was a deep love of physics. A classmate swore she heard them giggling in physics lab. They also loved being in the Rangers. Because they worked so well together, many project leaders requested them as a team. And McKnight recruited them for the HERO Team for exactly that reason.

"As you were," he said, returning their salutes. "Everyone get plenty of sleep?"

"Yes, sir," they replied.

He could read the truth on their faces.

They're as excited as I am.

Kathy Wu and Trevor George stood at the console, preparing for the time jump.

Trevor George was the last civilian hired for the Team. He had rusty brown hair and brown eyes. Before joining the team, he was a cold case investigator from the Atlanta Homicide Cold Case division. He played the saxophone and the electric bass guitar.

Trevor was called in to help with the team's first mission. General Drake and McKnight were so impressed by his deductive skills and analytical instincts, they offered him a position with the team. He took the job and moved to DC because of the opportunity to time travel and his budding affection for Kathy. They had moved in together a year before.

McKnight approached the console.

"Kathy, have we received a status from Major Tyler yet? Do we know where we'll be jumping to?"

"No, sir, but I'm expecting it any minute now."

"Very good." He rested his elbows on the platform side of the console. "I want to run something by you. The period costumes would help us blend in, but our overwhelming need is to convince Washington we're from the future, right?"

Kathy wrinkled her brow. "Yes. What are you suggesting?"

"I think we should wear our ACUs. We should look different and act like ourselves. What do you think?"

Kathy paused for a moment, then grinned.

"I'm irritated that I didn't think of that myself. But you should take the period clothes with you, just in case."

"Negative. With all our gear, they're excess baggage. We need to move fast. Besides, we won't be there long."

"Okay. I disagree, but it's your mission."

"Also, be ready for one of us to return by beacon, then jump back a few minutes later... for a time demo if we need one."

"Okay, sounds good. We're on it."

"Thanks, Kathy."

Smalls spoke to Hatcher and Wheeler, then came over to McKnight.

"I'm going to my office to change."

"No need. We're wearing our ACUs. I want Washington to feel we are different, and the ACUs will help."

"Yes, sir. I'll brief Hatcher and Wheeler. Is there anything else?"

"No," McKnight said. "Are you ready for this?"

Smalls shrugged. "As I'll ever be. It'll be fine. We got this."

"Good. Carry on."

"Yes, sir." Smalls saluted and went to brief Hatcher and Wheeler on the costume change.

"Colonel, I just heard from Major Tyler," Kathy said. "It's a five-by-five acknowledgement, and a position for your landing in 1787."

"Very good, Kathy. Thanks."

He turned to the others.

"Everything ready?"

The looks on their faces told the story. They were just waiting for the word. He motioned for them to gather around. When they did, he made eye contact with each of them.

"Remember, General Washington is a legendary figure who's done some great things, but he's just a man. Don't expect him to understand anything about electronic technology. As a gentleman farmer, he'll understand mechanics and some elementary physics. Questions about that?"

"No, sir!" they said in unison.

"And expect him to look different from the paintings we've seen. In those days, paintings always flattered the subject, or else the artist didn't get paid. And we treat him as a retired general, like General Drake. Are you with me?"

"Yes, sir!"

"And one more thing. Without us being there, Washington does his thing and gets the country off to a good start. We don't know what issues our presence will create. Therefore, no matter what else happens, we protect him at all costs while we are there. Everybody clear?"

"Yes, sir."

"Good. Kathy, do you have the coordinates plugged in yet?"

"Yes, sir. Everything's ready."

"Very good." He turned to the team. "If ever there was a mission where we should go by the book, it's this one. Kathy?"

"Green across the board," she said. "Line up here next to Trevor and get your beacons. Then we'll go."

Trevor and Kathy took each traveler through the preparation steps, with McKnight going last. As they completed their prep, each traveler took their place on the time engine platform.

McKnight felt the gravity of what they were doing. According to their charter, every time they jumped to a time space, they were required to avoid contact with the locals. This time, they were jumping to a pivotal age with orders to interact with a major player in history. Historical impact was guaranteed.

He pushed the thoughts away.

I'm a soldier. I follow orders.

He compartmentalized the dread and doubt, and joined his team, now all kneeling on the engine platform with a travel beacon hanging from their necks.

"Are you ready, team?" Kathy called out.

All travelers nodded.

Trevor picked up the trigger, thumbed up the trigger guard, and began the countdown.

"Target is Saturday, February 10th, 1787, at oh-nine hundred hours in the mountains of Virginia. Starting time jump in five… four… three… two… one… GO!"

The low hum of the time engine jumped up in volume and frequency. Time auras formed around each of them, then expanded to an enormous bubble around all of them. Particles in the air within the bubble ignited and spun furiously. Hatcher's ebony ponytail flew in all directions at once. Their clothing rippled as if they were inside a tornado.

The bubble bulged to twice its previous size and disappeared with a loud crack.

CHAPTER FIVE

Saturday, February 10th, 1787 - 8:00 AM EST - The Woods of Northern Virginia

The travelers fell through the familiar field of stars. McKnight saw the time bubble again. He could make out a clearing among trees and two shadowy figures beyond it.

The bubble bulged and dissipated. Major Tyler and Lieutenant Lagunas stood next to their landing point. McKnight steadied himself and stood. Smalls, Hatcher, and Wheeler did the same. Smalls pulled his waist pack open and dug into it.

Ah, the anti-nausea medication.

The time jump made some people ill. Tyler also experienced nausea every time he traveled.

Tyler and Lagunas walked over to the group.

"Report, Major," McKnight said.

"Yes, sir. General Washington and Mr. Lee are about a klick ahead of us on a trail up the mountain. They are on horseback, but setting a leisurely pace. Lieutenant Cutty is shadowing them from a half a klick behind."

"Good. Have you made contact?"

"No, sir. We were waiting for you." Tyler looked again at the new arrivals. "Sir, may I ask why you people are dressed in ACUs instead of period costume?"

"Sorry to spring that on you, Major. Kathy and I decided current battle dress would help us convince the General who we are. Does that screw up any tactics or plans you made?"

"No, sir. Makes sense, considering our goal. Are you ready to go chase a general across the mountains?"

"Yes, sir," Hatcher and Wheeler answered for McKnight.

"You bet," Smalls said.

"You heard the team, Major," McKnight said. "Let's move out."

"Lieutenant?" Tyler said to Lagunas, and she took off in the lead, setting a strong pace. Tyler and McKnight fell in behind her, followed by Smalls and Hatcher. Wheeler brought up the rear, turning around at intervals to check for threats.

McKnight scanned the surrounding forest while he ran. Fallen leaves provided a dull brown cover of the ground. There was frost in places. Winter in the Appalachian Mountains.

He didn't have to look at his team. He felt them all around him, working like a single organism. Pride swelled up within him.

This is what it's all about... Using our conditioning and brains to execute a mission.

They ran a kilometer before he saw Lagunas touch her left ear and raise her hand to slow the pace.

She's talking to Cutty.

Lagunas gave the stop signal.

Cutty stepped out of the trees and brush onto the trail. He appeared out of nowhere, like a ghost. It was a significant feat for a man his size.

He approached Lagunas. Tyler and McKnight joined them.

"The General is not too far ahead of us, sir," Cutty said. "But we have a problem. He's being followed. Looks like a group of eight to ten men. They aren't being very careful to hide themselves. Probably not military, certainly not professional... maybe a band of robbers. Maybe they saw the General in his nice clothes and have larceny or worse on their minds. Regardless, I think we should escalate our plans to ensure the General's safety."

"Agreed, Lieutenant," McKnight said. "Let's get closer and see what's what."

"Yes, sir. Follow me, sir."

Cutty took off at a blistering pace. The rest of the team matched his pace as they ran up the mountain after the trail of boot prints. Just over the top of the next rise, they stopped. Two dead men lay on the trail, one with a fatal sword wound, the other with gunpowder and a pistol wound in his chest.

"It looks like they dismounted here, sir," Cutty whispered. "The bandits must have caused them to stop somehow."

They heard shouting from downhill to the right. Cutty led them off the trail and in the direction of the voices. The heavy brush hid their approach. They stopped to assess the situation just outside a clearing.

There, before them, was a frightening scene. The bandits had tied Washington and Lee to a tree. Their horses stood in the trees beyond them, their reins dangling from their bridles. Another dead body lay just inside the clearing. Six angry men stood together before Washington, with one of them out front and holding the others back. He held Washington's sword in his hand.

Using hand signals, McKnight sent Hatcher and Smalls to one flank, and Lagunas and Wheeler to the other. He didn't have to caution them about lethal force. They all understood the implications of a death on the history path.

Did we cause this? Or did Washington experience it in history and talk his way out of it? Should I order my people to kill someone because they're threatening Washington? We can't wait and see if he's killed. We could fix a problem like that, but there's a real possibility that our government won't exist if he's killed, let alone the Lab and time travel technology. Then again, it would take some time for the time wave to reach our time...

Stop it! Read and analyze the situation.

McKnight focused on the conversation in the clearing.

"You're pretty good with this sword, Mister Gentleman," the leader said. "Got any military background, eh?"

Washington remained silent.

"I'm sure you're carrying more than this humble purse I found on your horse. Would you care to reveal the rest of your fortune? If you do, I'm happy to let you go with your life. We just need the money."

"Fergit that, David," one man said. "He's a gentleman and probably sided with the British. He's probably a bleedin' Tory. I say we kill him and get on with our business."

The leader turned on the man.

"You men elected me leader of this here band, Sam. As long as I am, we don't kill without reason. We're poor, not savages. We rob to survive. We don't kill without reason. Besides, I'm sure the gentleman will be cooperative." He turned back to Washington. "Won't you, sir?"

Before Washington could speak, McKnight and Tyler stepped out of the trees with their sidearms in their hands.

The robbers turned to them as McKnight spoke.

"Release him or you'll answer to us. This gentleman is our companion and under our protection."

The robbers spread out and raised their rifles.

"Just the two of you, then?" the leader said. "Not very good odds."

McKnight whistled, and the rest of the team stepped out of the bushes, weapons trained on the robbers. "I won't ask again. Lay down your weapons if you want to live."

The bandits laid down their weapons, but the one named Sam drew a knife, leaped toward Washington, and held the blade to his throat.

"I think you are the ones who should lie down your weapons. Else, I'll slice your benefactor's throat. Your choice."

McKnight didn't blink.

"Hatcher?" he said.

"No shot, sir, I'll hit the General."

"Cutty?"

"I have him, sir. Say the word and I'll blow his head off."

"Wait, now wait!" David cried out and stepped forward with his hands out.

"Hold, Sam!" he said, and pointed at Washington. "Did you call him General? Who is he?"

Tyler spoke. "That's General Washington. Did you fight with him during the war?"

Sam stepped away from Washington and dropped his knife.

"I did," he said. "I'm sorry, sir."

The other robbers hung their heads.

"We all did, sir," David said, dropping Washington's sword. "We wouldn't have attacked if we'd known it was you, sir. We'd sooner starve than hurt you."

Several of the others nodded.

Hatcher bounded over and cut the ropes that bound Washington and Lee to the tree, then went to secure the horses.

The general shrugged off the rope fragments, rubbed his wrists and, after a long look at Hatcher, he approached McKnight and Tyler.

"Sirs, I beg you, please release these men. Their primary crime is being hungry, a common plight in this part of the country. Three of them have already paid with their lives."

Before they could reply, Washington did a double-take and stared at Tyler's face.

"Colonel Tyler, isn't it?" he said. "You look different."

Tyler glanced at McKnight and winked with a smile.

McKnight could almost read his friend's mind and sense his humor. "I'm a colonel, too."

"Yes, General Washington. It's me. May I present—"

"I know," Washington said. "Colonel McKnight, I presume?"

McKnight was stunned. "How...?"

Washington looked him up and down.

"You're not what I expected, sir. I look forward to talking with you, but we have an immediate situation to resolve. What should we do with these men?"

David spoke up. "General Washington, you have our humblest apologies. We'll accept any punishment you demand. We deserve it."

Washington looked at McKnight, who gave a slight nod.

"When we were at war," Washington said, "I had men flogged for stealing."

He sighed.

"The war is over, and I'm a businessman now. I'm not inclined to punish these men. What about you, Colonel McKnight?"

"I'll leave it to you, General. It's to your discretion."

Washington nodded and turned back to the robbers. He walked to David and picked up his sword. He looked him in the eye, then stepped back to address all the bandits.

"I am releasing you to go back to your homes. If I learn you are waylaying people on this trail again, I shall raise a force and come looking for you. I won't be merciful the second time."

He approached the leader David again. The man stared at the ground.

Washington spoke in a low voice.

"Look at me, sir."

David raised his face to Washington. Tears flowed down his cheeks.

"These men respect you, David," Washington said. "You have influence over them. I'm counting on you to keep them on a Christian path. Don't let them stray."

"I will, sir," he said. "I swear before God I will."

"Good. Pick up your weapons and go home. Find a better way to survive if you can. If not, come see me at Mount Vernon. Together, we will find a solution."

David's men picked up their long guns and walked back uphill to the trail.

Washington turned his back to them and walked back to McKnight and Tyler.

McKnight glanced at Wheeler, who nodded and slipped into the brush after the robbers.

Washington looked at Tyler again. He touched Tyler's hat and said, "May I?"

"Yes, sir," Tyler said, and Washington reached forward and lifted his hat from his head.

"I've known you for twenty years now, Colonel, and the last time I saw you, your hairline was receding. Now your hair is full again and the wrinkles on your face are gone. How is this possible?"

"It's part of a plan, sir," Tyler said. "It's what brought us here to this time and place."

"A plan?" Washington said. "Clearly, there's more here than I perceive."

He turned to McKnight.

"So, tell me, Colonel McKnight, what army are you in? What brings you and your men..." He stopped and scanned the faces before him, his eyes resting on Hatcher and Lagunas. "... Your men and women... to these woods?"

"We represent the Army of the United States, sir, and we came here looking for you."

Washington nodded. "It appears you have found me, Colonel. What can I do for you?"

McKnight laughed. "That we have, sir. We need your help, and if you'll allow me a few minutes of your time, I'll explain."

Washington looked around and spread out his arms.

"I am at your disposal, Colonel. How can I help?"

CHAPTER SIX

Saturday, February 10th, 1787 - 11:30 AM - The Woods of Northern Virginia

"General Washington, I understand you have questions," McKnight said. "And I promise you, I will answer all of them. But first, I noticed you have a cut on your left arm. Is it from your encounter with the bandits?"

Washington glanced at his arm. "So there is." He looked back at McKnight. "I didn't notice. I presumed I had escaped unscathed."

"We should get a dressing on that before we do anything else. Captain Wheeler?"

Wheeler jumped forward. "Yes, sir?"

"Get the medkit and dress the General's wound, please."

"Yes, sir," Wheeler said. He shrugged off his backpack and opened it.

While he dug out the medkit, McKnight spoke again.

"DNA sample as well."

"Yes, sir."

McKnight turned back to Washington.

"Sir, first… may I ask how you knew my name?"

Washington looked surprised.

"Why, I expected Colonel Tyler would have told you he mentioned your name to me. He promised to introduce me to you someday when you were in the area. When you and he arrived to help us in the nick of time, I supposed you must be the man he told me about."

McKnight glanced at Tyler, who grinned back at him.

"Well, you were correct, sir. I expected he would mention my name, but I didn't know he already had."

"I see," Washington said.

He glanced around, taking in the team and their uniforms. "If you please, Colonel McKnight… what army are you part of and where do you come from? Your uniforms and armament are strange to me, and your speech is very informal."

McKnight noticed Will Lee was standing behind Washington with his head bowed.

"Will Lee," he said. "Please come forward and stand next to your master. This concerns you, too."

Lee raised his head and looked at Washington, who gestured for him to come forward. Lee stepped up in line with his master.

McKnight motioned for the team to line up in front of Washington.

When they were in position, Tyler said, "Ten Hut!"

The team snapped to attention, then relaxed as Tyler put them at ease.

McKnight smiled at his team. He couldn't have been prouder.

"General Washington, I present to you the Historical Event Research Organization Team from the 75th Regimental Special Troops Battalion of the United States Army. The 75th Regiment is better known as the Army Rangers."

"You're from Rogers' Rangers?" Washington said.

McKnight glanced at the team, then back at Washington. "No, sir, I think our origins come more from John Mosby and Francis Marion."

Washington looked at Tyler. "You were with General Marion when I met you, Colonel. That is how we became acquainted."

"Yes, sir," Tyler said, "but I was already in this unit before I joined General Marion."

"Yes, he introduced you as the finest combat trainer he had ever met." Washington looked thoughtful. "How old are you, Colonel?"

"I was thirty-three in September, sir."

Washington looked confused. "I know you enlisted with General Marion during the war with the French. That was twenty-five years ago. You would have been eight years old. I saw you myself four years ago at Fraunces Tavern in New York, and you looked older than you do now. How is that possible?"

"It isn't, sir, unless you have conquered time itself," McKnight said. "I guess there is no easy way to explain this, so I'll just say it and then try to prove it to you. We came here this morning from the distant future. When were you born, Major Tyler?"

"September 23th, sir. In the year of our Lord 2003."

"And where did you grow up?"

"I was born in Atlanta, Georgia. I attended Riverside Academy in Gainesville, Georgia. Then I was accepted into the United States Military Academy at West Point in the spring of 2021."

Washington's face flushed.

"Sir, I do not appreciate your attempt at humor. You suggest magic exists, and I know it does not. Only God can step through time."

McKnight nodded. "General Washington, believe me, I understand your skepticism. With the utmost respect for you, sir, I beg your indulgence for a few minutes. Give me a chance to prove we are who we say we are."

Washington stood in silence for a moment. When he spoke, it was in a measured tone.

"You saved my life a few minutes ago, Colonel McKnight. For that, I owe you at least a few minutes of my attention. However, if at the end of that time I am still unconvinced, I ask that we speak no further of it. I am a Christian man, and I choose not to expose myself to anything that isn't consistent with my faith. Can we agree on that?"

"Yes, sir. I will not ask you to believe anything that goes against your faith. I am a Christian myself. What I will show you are advances in science that don't exist in 1787 but are possible in my time. I promise you; I will give you proof we come from a society later than the eighteenth century."

Washington looked at the faces of the HERO Team. McKnight followed his eyes to look at his own people. He could see on their faces their wish for Washington to believe.

"We will talk about it again in ten minutes," Washington said. "What do you have to show me?"

"Lieutenant Cutty?" McKnight said. "Front and center."

Cutty dashed to stand at attention next to McKnight.

"At ease, Lieutenant. General Washington, how long does it take to load and fire a Brown Bess?"

Washington blinked. "In defensive positions or offensive positions?"

"Defensive is faster, isn't it, sir?"

"Yes," Washington said, "About twenty to thirty seconds, depending on the skill of the soldier."

"Yes, sir. Given that information, it takes two minutes to load and fire six times, doesn't it? And what about the accuracy, sir?"

"Good at close range. Questionable over thirty yards."

"I agree, sir." McKnight looked up the mountain slope and searched the trees. "Lieutenant Cutty, do you see the oak tree there with the broken limb about thirty yards out?"

"Yes, sir."

"On my command, I want you to put six rounds in that tree at the base of the broken limb."

"Yes, sir." Cutty raised his M4A1 and aimed at the spot.

McKnight turned to Washington. "Sir, if you will focus on the spot on the tree I mentioned, Lieutenant Cutty will demonstrate the capabilities of our standard issue combat weapon."

"I will," he said.

I've got his attention. He can't hide the interest in his eyes.

McKnight turned back to Cutty.

"Fire." The word barely left his lips before Cutty discharged his weapon.

Pop! Pop! Pop! Pop! Pop! Pop!

McKnight turned to Washington. "Sir, how much time was that, from start to finish?"

Washington looked stunned. "It… it must have been less than three seconds," he said.

McKnight gestured to Washington to accompany him, and they walked to the tree. All of Cutty's shots struck the tree within two inches of each other.

Washington examined the impact point, turned to McKnight, and shook his head.

"If I had not seen it with my own eyes…" He looked down the hill at Cutty. "I have never met a soldier who could shoot this accurately, to say nothing of the time required to reload. How was he able to shoot six times with such results without reloading?"

"Today, in 1787, he could not, sir. I'll grant you Lieutenant Cutty is a fine marksman, but the weapon's technology is responsible for transferring his skill to the results with accuracy. In the future, ammunition makers will learn to put the wadding and ball into a metal shell that is of a consistent size and shape. That makes it easier to load. Then they created mechanical systems to load the weapon faster. And they learned to rifle the barrel so that the bullet spins."

"What does that mean?" Washington said.

McKnight waved Cutty forward.

"Lieutenant, show the General a bullet from your weapon."

Cutty did as instructed.

Washington turned the bullet over in his hand, then held it up to the light.

"How could a ball fit into this… metal shell?"

"The lead projectile is smaller and oblong-shaped," Cutty said. "But trust me, sir, the accuracy and velocity of the projectile make up for the size."

"And the… what did you call it? Rifling?"

"Yes, sir," McKnight said. "Lieutenant? Dissemble your weapon so the General can see the rifling in the barrel."

"Yes, sir."

Cutty broke down his weapon and offered the barrel to Washington. "Careful, sir," he said. "The barrel is still a little warm."

Washington nodded, pointed the barrel upward, and peered through it. "I see curving lines inside the barrel. Is that what you call rifling?"

"Yes, sir. The weapon is called a rifle… well, a carbine actually. Instead of a ball, the projectile is oblong, so it doesn't tumble out of the barrel like a ball does. Tumbling reduces the accuracy. The lines in the barrel cause the projectile to spin, which makes it fly truer."

"No weapon maker can do that."

"No, sir," McKnight said. "Not today. But they learn how in the future."

"That is astounding."

"Yes, it is, sir, from your point of view in history." He gestured to Washington to walk with him back to the team.

"I'd like an opportunity to shoot one when possible, sir," Washington said.

"Of course. I'll arrange for you to shoot one and practice with it. In the meantime, let me show you something else."

"I must admit I am intrigued, Colonel McKnight. You have my complete attention."

"Thank you. Now, may I ask you, sir? How do members of a force communicate during a battle?"

Washington shook his head. "They don't. This is a problem during battle. You can lay the best plans, but no plan holds together once you encounter the enemy. As a commander, you don't know what is happening, and you can't get the word to your men, even if you do." He thought for a moment. "Well, of course, we use hand signals when the forces are in line of sight, and runners when they are close, but not much more."

"I see," McKnight said. "Let me show you something."

They reached the team.

"General Washington, please select one of my team."

Washington looked at them and pointed to Hatcher. "This young lady, if you please."

"Captain Hatcher, front and center."

Hatcher dashed to position in front of them and saluted Washington.

Washington returned her salute, then looked back and forth between McKnight and Hatcher. "She... she's an officer?"

"Yes, sir. And well earned. Captain Hatcher is one of the best hand-to-hand combat warfighter I know. And I know quite a few."

"She goes into battle?"

The look on Hatcher's face expressed her irritation.

McKnight nodded at her, then pointed in her direction. "Sir, she's an officer in the United States Army and can speak for herself."

"Very well," Washington said. "Captain... Hatcher, is it?"

"Yes, sir."

"I beg your pardon, Captain, if I have committed an impropriety. Please forgive me."

"I'm not offended, sir. What would you like to know?"

"Thank you, I am humbled by your graciousness. Tell me, Captain, where did you get your officer training? Were you promoted in the field?"

"No, sir. I received my commission upon graduation from the University of North Georgia in the year 2031. My degrees are in mathematics and physics."

"Mathematics, I'm familiar with. What is physics... to you, I mean?"

"I remain a student of modern physics, sir. It has at its roots the works of Newton, Galileo, Archimedes, and Copernicus, among others."

"I'm not familiar with their writings," Washington said. "But I've heard some of those names from my good friend Madison." He turned to McKnight. "What did you want to show me?"

"A communications demonstration, sir. A way to communicate with your troops in a combat situation. Sir, please walk into the trees on the other side of the clearing with Captain Hatcher. Make sure you are out of ear shot and line of sight. Once there, give her a phrase to send to me. When you return, I will tell you what she said."

Washington looked to the clearing and the trees, then back at McKnight.

"Just the two of us?"

"I beg your pardon, sir?" McKnight said.

"He means without a chaperone, Colonel," Hatcher said, and turned to Washington. "Respectfully, General Washington, no man could have his way with me without my permission. But I believe with all my heart I have nothing to fear from you. You and I don't need a chaperone."

Washington looked amazed.

"Whatever else is true, your culture differs from mine. But if you don't feel the need for a chaperone, Captain Hatcher, we can proceed."

He turned to McKnight.

"I estimate the clearing is forty yards away, and we will be on the other side of it. How can you do this?"

"With this." McKnight held up his PNR radio. He pointed at Hatcher, and she held up hers as well.

Washington looked puzzled but walked with Hatcher until they disappeared in the woods beyond the clearing.

McKnight's radio crackled. "Sir, can you read me?" Hatcher said.

"Five by five, Captain," he said.

"Just a moment, sir."

McKnight could hear Hatcher talking to Washington. "Just speak in a whisper, sir, and Colonel McKnight will hear you."

She's turning it over to him. Good idea.

Washington's voice came through loud and clear.

Washington and Hatcher returned to where the team stood.

"Well, Colonel?" Washington said. "What message did you receive?"

McKnight smiled. "A great message indeed, sir. 'For God so loved the world, he gave his only begotten Son.'"

Washington looked from McKnight to Hatcher. "How was that possible? How does it work?"

McKnight held up his PNR radio. "It is done with technology you don't have yet, sir."

"If I had that during the war..." Washington said. "What is the range of this?"

"In our time, there is supporting equipment that increases the range. Without it, the range is about two-thirds of a mile."

Washington nodded. "That would be very useful if the battle is small and close by. What about larger battles? Or battle news from another state?" he said.

"Sir, with some additional equipment, we can extend the range hundreds of miles. It's all about the technology and the power to run it."

"Power?"

"Yes, sir. You're familiar with the work Mr. Franklin has done with electricity?"

Washington pulled at his chin.

"Only in passing. A few anecdotes, that's all. I know there's a connection between electricity and lightning, but I don't see how it can be useful because you cannot control it."

McKnight nodded and opened his radio to expose the battery.

"See here, sir? This is a battery. It stores electricity and makes this mechanism possible. I don't completely understand the science behind it... but I don't need to, because others made the technology into a tool I can use. May I offer an analogy? You learned the business of warfare from both your enemies and your allies, and they learned it from their fathers and grandfathers. You made mistakes but learned from them. What you learned over the years helped you to defeat the British during the war."

Washington nodded and looked him in the eye. "I understand this analogy, I think. Many people experimented with electricity, then shared what they learned. Others took that knowledge, experimented, and learned more. Each step allows further steps. Is that what you mean?"

"Exactly, sir. You have it. There's one more dynamic at work. The more we learn, the faster societies can adapt the technology to be useful. Further experimentation is done and technologies are combined to create new innovations, and the pace of technical advancement increases. In fact, Mr. Franklin took one of the first steps toward electrical power by capturing an electric charge in a jar."

"I see." Washington said. "You make a compelling case for your technology and how it comes from science rather than... elsewhere. Give me a moment to reflect, Colonel."

"Of course, sir."

He gestured to his valet. "Will, walk with me."

They walked far enough away for privacy and turned their backs toward the team. A snowy Virginia valley stretched out before them.

It occurred to McKnight that Washington might ask Will Lee for his opinion. While he could not see their lips, their postures suggested Lee did most of the talking while Washington listened.

He saw Washington turn to Lee. They both nodded and walked back to the group.

"If I may, Colonel," Washington said, "I'd like to ask you some questions."

"Of course, sir. You've been more than patient with us. What can I answer for you?"

I'm about to find out if Washington believes my story.

Washington paused as if he expected McKnight to say more. When he didn't, Washington continued.

"You say you are from the future. Do you mean to say I am part of your history?"

"Yes, sir."

"So the things you showed me... the technology... will be a reality someday in my time?"

I've got to be careful here. I don't want to give him foreknowledge of events here in his time... yet.

"No, sir. There will be advances during your life, but these things take time. Ideas are born, theories are tested, and then there must be manufacturing and distribution in quantity. Once the new thing is available, new ideas spring forth. In short, it takes a long time, but the process accelerates as people solve technical problems."

McKnight shrugged and raised his hands, palms upward. "Sorry," he said. "That was a long answer to a simple question."

"I appreciate your candor, sir," Washington said. He glanced at Lee, then continued. "I'm convinced your weaponry is far superior to anything I know of." He waved at the HERO Team. "And I'm also convinced that your team and its weaponry could fend off attacks from a contemporary force many times larger, correct?"

"As you know better than most, General, nothing is certain in battle," McKnight said. "But all other things being equal, the answer is yes."

Washington grunted. "Spoken like a cautious man who has led soldiers into combat. If I heard your story yesterday without the benefit of these demonstrations, I would have declared the tale rubbish and the teller insane." He spread his arms. "And yet, here you are. I have seen much in my life, and I have learned to trust my own eyes and ears."

He wants to believe us.

"All that said, I remain skeptical. This is the year of our Lord, 1787. From where did you come? Or perhaps a better question is, from when did you come?"

He's learning.

"Thank you, General. We journeyed here on this same date from the year 2037."

Washington and Lee glanced at each other, then Washington spoke.

"That is 250 years from now, Colonel. What in the world could you possibly want from me? What could I do for you that you couldn't do for yourself with your advanced weaponry and technology?"

"That's a good question, sir, and now we can discuss that in context. First of all, we are not here to ask for your advice in military matters."

He looked over his shoulder at the HERO Team. They were still standing at ease behind him.

"As you were, everyone." He glanced at his watch. "Major Tyler, please set up a camp and get some food prepared while the General and I chat."

"Yes, sir." Tyler turned to the team. "You heard the man. Snap to it."

CHAPTER SEVEN

Saturday, February 10th, 1787 - 12:14 PM - The Woods of Northern Virginia

McKnight turned back to Washington.

"There's a question you didn't ask me, General, and I expected it to be the first thing you asked once you believed we are who we say we are. I—"

"I haven't said I believe you yet, Colonel," Washington interrupted, then held up his hand. "Do not take offense, sir, but I'm comparing what I know to be true and what you've said. My mind is open because I know I can see a mountain and not yet know what lies beyond. I'm still listening."

"Thank you, sir. I apologize for assuming a fact without you affirming it in advance."

Washington nodded at McKnight. "Apology accepted, Colonel. What else do you have to show me?"

"General, I think it's time we show you how we travel through time."

"That, I would like to see, Colonel. What are you going to do?"

"Whom should I send, sir? I don't want you to feel I have staged some type of trickery."

"I think I'm beyond that, Colonel McKnight. You pick the man… or woman."

"Very well, sir." McKnight scanned the team. They were busy setting up camp and getting a fire started.

"Major Smalls?" he said. "May we have a moment?"

"Of course, sir," Smalls said, and walked to General Washington and McKnight.

Washington's eyes widened. "A Negro? An officer?"

A frown flashed across Smalls' face, then disappeared.

"Of course, sir," McKnight said. "He has earned his rank through his service in numerous engagements. Major Smalls was part of a specialized, highly trained organization within the United States Military before he joined our team. He was a Navy SEAL. SEAL stands for sea, air, and land, which are the places where they operate. The SEAL Team chooses only the very best men and women."

Smalls came to attention and saluted. "At your service, General Washington. How can I help?"

Washington looked at Smalls, and then back at McKnight. "You said sea, air, and land, Colonel. I understand men trained to fight on land, and I can guess about fighting at sea, but in the air? How is that possible?"

McKnight shook his head. "General, there is much about the future we haven't shared with you, and it must remain a mystery until and unless you agree to help us. For now, let's ignore that question and jump ahead to the time travel demonstration. That's the most important thing for you to see. If I may?"

Washington stared at McKnight for a few seconds.

I just made him suspicious. I should have held off about the SEAL Team.

"Let's proceed for now, Colonel," Washington said. "But I do wish to come back to this topic."

"Yes, sir," McKnight said, but hesitated.

I can't let this hang. I need to set him at ease.

"General Washington, I apologize, because I ignored your curiosity to move faster. May I explain?"

"Yes, sir. Please."

McKnight considered how to start.

The only approach I can use with this man is direct and total honesty.

"Sir, in the year 1903, two brothers will demonstrate that an object heavier than air can fly. They learned to harness air pressure to achieve flight."

"Is this true? If so, it is nothing short of amazing. What do you mean by air pressure?"

"Sir, you experience air pressure every time the wind blows. Have you ever experienced a high wind that threatened to knock you off your feet? Or a severe storm at sea?"

"Yes, of course."

"Sir, that is air pressure in nature, with no controls or redirection. Can you imagine if it was focused, magnified, and harnessed to create force to do work?"

"I think I see what you mean," Washington said.

"I hope that explanation helps reduce your distress, sir. And now you might realize why I omitted it. In 250 years, man has learned much. We could spend hours discussing advances in science, or we could show you how we got here."

Washington pulled at his chin and nodded. "I see your point, Colonel. Please continue with your demonstration."

"Thank you, sir," McKnight said, and turned to Smalls.

"Major, we discussed a demo of the time engine for General Washington. Please ask Doctor Wu to recall you to the present, then send you back to this spot after..." He looked at Washington. "What do you think, General? Send him back here after one minute?"

"Yes," Washington said. "Surely that is long enough to prove your point?"

"Yes, sir!" Smalls said, and saluted Washington. "I'm on it, sir." Smalls began tapping away on his phone.

McKnight touched Washington on the shoulder. "We should step back, sir, unless you're thinking you'd like to go with him."

Washington turned toward McKnight. He must have realized McKnight was joking, because he smiled, and they both stepped back a few yards.

"We're on," Smalls said, and kneeled on the ground.

Washington leaned toward McKnight and whispered. "Why is he kneeling?"

"There's a force that pushes you backwards when you arrive in a new time. We don't know why, but if you're standing, the pull can take you off your feet. If you're kneeling, the pull is still strong, but less likely to put you on the ground."

"I see."

"Safe travels, Major," McKnight said.

"Thank you, sir," Smalls said.

A blue aura surrounded him. When he shifted his weight, the aura shifted with him. It became brighter until Smalls was hard to see.

"Is he in danger? Washington said.

"No. Not with his training. He'll be safe."

Smalls' aura grew brilliant, flared, and he and the light disappeared.

Washington stepped back in amazement, then composed himself. Will Lee stood next to him with his mouth wide open.

"Okay, he's gone back to the future, General. He'll be back in one minute."

Washington and Lee approached the place where Smalls knelt. They squatted together and touched the ground. Lee looked up at the trees.

"Gentlemen, he is not here. He will return in a few seconds. Please step back from where he was. He'll return to the same spot, and it's dangerous to be there when he does."

Lee and Washington retreated from the spot.

McKnight looked at his watch. "He should be back here in about twenty seconds."

Washington stood by McKnight. Lee stood behind him but moved aside so he could watch Smalls' return.

"Okay," McKnight said. "It's been about a minute. He should return any second now."

Fifteen seconds passed, but Smalls didn't return.

What could be keeping him? Is there a problem with the engine?

Washington touched McKnight's sleeve. "Do you think something is wrong, Colonel?"

"No, sir," he said. "There are a couple of generals waiting for us to return. One of them may have asked Major Smalls for a report. It would be hard for them not to ask what's happening and if he believed you would help us. That wouldn't surprise me at all."

Washington grunted. "I guess we'll see in a moment, won't we?" he said. "How long has he been gone?"

McKnight checked his watch. "Almost two minutes. He should be back soon, sir."

What could be the holdup?

He glanced at Washington.

He has to be growing more suspicious by the second.

Then an aura appeared, filled with the silhouette of a kneeling man. McKnight sighed with relief.

The aura brightened, then disappeared, leaving Smalls kneeling on the ground. He jumped up and walked to McKnight and Washington. When he came to attention in front of them, Washington stepped forward and reached out to touch him.

Smalls extended his hand for Washington to touch. Lee sprang forward to touch him as well.

"Yes, it's me, sir. I'm not a phantasm or a magic trick. I traveled 250 years to the future and back. And I brought something back with me." From under his arm, he drew a newspaper and handed it to McKnight. "I'm sorry, sir, for the delay. When I landed in the lab, it occurred to me that a newspaper from our era might interest the General. It took a little longer than expected to find one. I had to get one at the front desk of the building."

"Thank you, Major. It's okay. I'm irritated I didn't think of it myself."

McKnight turned to Washington and waved the newspaper at him. "Sir, I have reservations about showing this to you because we shouldn't be revealing the future. But I owe you truth and clarity about what we're asking of you before you can agree to it."

He glanced at Lee, then turned back to Washington.

"Sir, my history tells me you're renowned for keeping your word. But I don't know Mr. Lee well enough to know about his integrity. Will you vouch for him?"

"Will? Wait a moment." Washington turned to Lee. "Come here, Will."

Lee approached McKnight and Washington.

"I'm giving my word to Colonel McKnight, Will, that I will repeat nothing I have learned or will learn today. I'm asking you to do the same. Will you give your word to him as well?"

Lee nodded. "Yes, sir, I will. I have heard many secret discussions, and you know I have always kept my mouth shut and my thoughts to myself unless you asked for them."

"An accurate statement, Will. I have never known you to betray a trust or a confidence."

He turned back to McKnight.

"Is that good enough for you, Colonel? Will and I agree to remain silent about anything you share with us."

"Thank you, sir," McKnight said. "One additional thought. Newspapers have declined in our time. Most of us get our current events from this..." He pulled out his phone and held it up. "Newspaper companies have moved to electronic distribution of their content. Today's content is mostly opinion. It should be a strict reporting of the news, but it isn't. Does that make sense?"

"Yes, it does. That statement applies to newsletters in this time as well. But I'll keep what you said in mind as I read it."

"Very good, sir," he said, and handed the newspaper to Washington.

As the man fumbled in his pockets for his reading glasses, Lee craned his neck for a look at the paper.

"I'm not sure how to ask this," McKnight said. "And I hope you'll understand that I mean no offense…"

"What is it, Colonel? Please say what you mean."

"Thank you, sir. I wanted to ask… I mean, I… Sir, can Mr. Lee read?"

"That is a relevant question, Colonel. Yes, he can. I taught him myself while we've traveled together. I trust him, and I wanted him to read and comment on letters I have received and letters I have written. It makes my correspondence much easier."

Washington examined the paper. "This is better quality than the newsletters I've seen." He hesitated. "But you said newsletters have declined in your time?"

"Yes, sir, but it was the only type of news document Major Smalls could bring across time. Most news devices require support systems that doesn't exist here. But some people in our time prefer to hold a newspaper in their hands while they read, so they are still available."

"What does this line mean?" Lee said. "It says Washington is embroiled in scandal."

Washington scanned the front page. "That is discouraging. Is this Washington a… descendant of mine who is less than discreet?"

McKnight looked at Smalls, who shrugged.

.

CHAPTER EIGHT

"I don't think so, sir," McKnight said. "This is why I was reluctant to show the paper to you. But perhaps it's for the best. In 1790, the United States government will establish a city on the northern banks of the Potomac River to serve as its capital. Sir, they named it after you. People in our time use the name Washington to refer to both the town and the government. This headline suggests that someone has discovered a scandal in the government."

Washington stared at the paper. "I want to read this and try to understand your culture better."

McKnight shook his head. "Respectfully, sir, Major Smalls brought this paper to show you more proof of who we are. Unless you decide to work with us on our... issue, it's not in your best interest to know too much about the future. I think you'll agree when you consider our earlier discussion about changing history."

Washington frowned and looked back and forth between McKnight and Smalls. "This doesn't engender confidence and trust in our relationship, Colonel."

McKnight shifted his weight. He realized he had stood still long enough that his body became stiff with the cold.

"Yes, General, I know. If you will allow me to explain why we're here, it will be clear to you why it's a bad idea at this point in time."

Washington handed the paper to McKnight.

"Very well, sir," he said. "Please allow Will and me a moment to discuss this."

"Certainly, sir," McKnight said.

The General and Lee walked away up the trail. They stopped and sat on a log along the path.

Smalls moved closer to McKnight. "I'm sorry, sir," he said. "I didn't realize the newspaper would cause such a turmoil."

McKnight shrugged. "No, it was a good idea, after all. We'll have to get used to minor questions that require long answers."

"I think this is going to be harder than we thought."

"Yes, I believe you're right, Major."

After a moment, McKnight said, "Check with Tyler and get that document package from him."

"Yes, sir," Smalls said, saluted, and turned away to find Tyler.

Yes, it's going to be harder than we thought.

He watched Washington from where he stood. Washington noticed and waved. McKnight interpreted his posture and expression as a signal.

Give me a few more minutes.

Tyler and Smalls returned with the document package.

"Are you going to let him see it, sir?" Tyler asked. "Are you sure it's wise?"

"No, I'm not sure," McKnight said. "But I don't see another way to go forward. If we want his cooperation and his trust, we have to give him something. The newspaper is too confusing. But he knows about the issues and problems of his time, and he knows the movers and shakers. This document comes from his time. Hopefully, it will speak for itself and ring true."

"Yes, sir." Tyler turned his gaze to Washington and Lee.

"They're coming back."

Washington nodded at Tyler and spoke to McKnight.

"Sir, you have shown us things we have never seen before. Your weaponry and demonstration of time travel are beyond our reach. You've piqued my curiosity. I'd like to know why you're here. Please enlighten us."

McKnight nodded and smiled. "Thank you for your patience and forbearance, sir. I'll be brief, and then we can discuss details."

He glanced at Smalls and Tyler and began again.

"Sir, you're meeting in Philadelphia soon to work with others to address flaws and suggest amendments to the Articles of Confederation, are you not?"

Washington met McKnight's eyes. "How do you know that, sir?"

"My history books tell me, General," McKnight said. "But you are aware that fixing the Articles won't be enough, correct?"

Washington stared at McKnight.

"Even if you fix them, sir," McKnight continued, "the central government won't be strong enough to manage the defense of the states. Continuing under the Articles would result in an America that looks like Europe — a group of quarreling states that fight over petty issues and can't protect themselves from larger, predatory nations."

Washington said nothing for a long second. When he spoke again, his voice was quiet and measured. "You have remarkable perception, Colonel. What are you suggesting?"

"It's not perception, sir. It's hindsight. You and others — most notably Hamilton, Madison, and Jay — will help the state delegations understand the Articles are insufficient and a more comprehensive founding document is necessary."

"Are you suggesting I do that? That I organize these men to reform the Articles?"

"No, sir. I'm saying you've already come to that conclusion yourself, or will come to it soon. We don't want you to do anything differently than you have already decided."

"Then what do you need from me?" Washington said.

McKnight waved the package at Washington. "Before you look at it, let me tell you why we are here." He glanced around. "We should sit down. This might take a while."

"Let's move back to the camp, sir," Tyler said. "We've set up a little conference area."

"Good. After you, General."

They walked to the team's bivouac and sat on blankets arranged in a circle. McKnight sat cross-legged on one blanket. Washington sat in front of him, and the others gathered around.

"In a nutshell, our government is in turmoil. My President sent us here. He believes our government has forgotten the reasons you and your fellow patriots felt it necessary to revise the Articles."

McKnight handed the package to Washington.

"Don't open it yet, sir. These documents are copies of the actual plan you and your colleagues create in Philadelphia. There are three branches of the government — an executive branch headed by a President, a legislative branch with two houses, and a judicial branch. The plan was for each of the three branches to have controls that limit the power of the other two. Does that make sense, sir?"

"Yes, it does. We've had some correspondence about this approach." Washington leaned forward. "Are you saying there's a problem with it?"

"No, sir. It works pretty well for many years, but over the last sixty years, the legislature has ceded power to the executive branch so the President can issue executive orders to wield power beyond his office."

"So he can act as a king?" Washington asked.

"After a fashion, sir. If one political party has control of Congress and agrees with the President, it's hard to reverse his executive orders—"

"Damned political parties!" Washington said and looked at Lee. "Haven't I said they would cause problems?"

"Yes, sir," Lee said.

Washington looked back at the soldiers before him and hesitated. After a moment, he spoke again.

"Ladies and gentlemen, please forgive my outburst and my profanity. I am vehemently opposed to anyone that puts loyalty to their party above the people of our nation."

"Many feel the same way in our time, sir," McKnight said. "More troubling, though, is the suspected collusion between the political parties. Some believe the political parties work together to stay in power, creating an American royalty — a class of politicians that are unassailable and spend their time fighting over power instead of solving the country's problems."

Washington's face was ashen. "Are all our efforts in vain, then?"

"No, sir. There are many who want to fix these issues. Among them are the President who sent us, my commanding officer, and many citizens. But the President can't do it alone, and there are many in the government who want him to fail."

"Are political parties to blame for this?"

"They probably have some culpability, but it's natural for people to gather around a cause or a personality. It may have more to do with the people attracted to politics. I don't know, but there are people in both parties who have compromised the integrity of the government."

"I don't see how I can help with that."

"I'm getting to that, sir. The country has become so divided that many people have taken up arms and we are one misstep or political miscalculation away from civil war. We're trying to avoid this. There is one thing you have, sir, that others don't."

"And what is that, pray tell?"

"Credibility, sir. As you were a leader in our revolt against England, you will become a leader for our new nation. Many Americans consider you the father of our nation. We believe the people of our time respect you enough to listen. We want you to meet with our Congress, the President, and the Judiciary. Then we'd like to introduce you to the people."

Washington stared into McKnight's eyes. "Am I to read a speech prepared by your President?"

McKnight shook his head. "No, sir. He assured us you can say whatever you like, and I agree with him. What you put together has lasted for many years. He wants you to explain to the public—our public—how Americans feel in 1787, and why the government was organized as it was. He believes... *we* believe... that you can help the Americans in 2037 remember what's been forgotten and help our government recover to its original form and function."

"I see," Washington said.

"Thanks for your patience, sir. Now, it's time to open the document package."

Washington unwrapped the package and found a box with several documents in it.

"You'll want to keep the contents of this to yourself, General," McKnight said. "It is a copy of the new constitution you and your colleagues will produce in Philadelphia in the spring, along with the first ten amendments."

"Do you mean this as a guide for us? Are you saying this is what we should do?"

"No, sir. I'm saying that it's what our history tells us you and your colleagues develop on your own. I'm suggesting that you read it... or don't. Whatever you decide to do, put the document aside afterwards and don't look at it again until after your convention. When it is over, pull this document out and see how closely it matches the results. I suggest it is the ultimate proof that we are who we say we are."

Tyler appeared at McKnight's side.

"Sir, I have something you need to see."

McKnight glanced at him. "Can't it wait? We're in the middle of something here."

"Yes, sir, I know. But you *really* need to see this."

The tone in Tyler's voice stopped him. He turned and saw the urgency in Tyler's eyes.

"Very well."

He turned back to Washington.

"Sir, would you excuse me for a few minutes?"

"Certainly, Colonel," Washington said. "What you've said makes sense to me, as far as it goes. I've decided I'll read through this document for a sense of what it contains. Then I'll put it away until after the convention."

McKnight nodded. "That's a wise choice, sir. If I were in your shoes, I'd do the same."

Washington nodded, stood, and walked away from the bivouac, carrying the documents.

McKnight stood and fell in step with Tyler.

"Okay. What's so damned important that it couldn't wait?"

"A dead body, sir."

"A what?"

"A body, sir. A dead man."

"People died in this age, too, right? What makes this one so different you needed to interrupt my discussion with General Washington?"

"Sir, we don't think this body belonged to anyone from 1787."

McKnight stopped in his tracks. Tyler stopped as well.

They exchanged eye contact. No further discussion was required.

McKnight started walking again, faster this time.

"Show me."

CHAPTER NINE

Tyler headed back to the trail. He looked back over his shoulder at McKnight. "Cutty found it while checking the perimeter of the camp. He alerted Major Smalls, who told me. Smalls and Cutty are still with the body, sir. It's about a hundred meters out."

McKnight followed him uphill. They came upon Smalls and Cutty, standing together, looking at something on the ground.

It was a grisly scene. The head and a shoulder were missing. A forearm and hand, apparently from the missing shoulder, laid by the body. The wound was charred. The smell of burnt flesh wafted up from the body.

McKnight looked around on the ground.

Smalls knelt by the body.

Where's the head and shoulder?

"It's not here, sir," Smalls said. "You're looking for the head, right?" He pointed at Cutty. "We've been checking around the area — ten meters in all directions."

"I doubt we'll find it, Colonel," Tyler said. "I think it's—"

"Yeah, yeah," McKnight said, and rolled his eyes. "*How* could that be the case, Major?"

Smalls grunted, then said, "Lieutenant Cutty?"

"Yes, sir?"

"Go back to the camp, make sure General Washington and Mr. Lee are comfortable, and relay to Captain Wheeler to organize some chow. Make sure the General gets to try an MRE. We'll be there shortly."

"Yes, sir!" Cutty said. He turned and ran down the hill.

When Cutty was out of earshot, Smalls stood.

"This man was about six foot five, give or take an inch. A big boy, by any standards. If he was unaware of the time bubble dangers… *this* could be the result, right?"

"Okay," McKnight said. "What do we know about him?"

"Not much, but enough," Smalls continued. "The clothes aren't from this time. Much more modern. He's Caucasian. Maybe a teenager. He hasn't been dead more than an hour. Otherwise, the wolves or some other critters would have gotten to the body. There are some ants, but not much else. No, he hasn't been here long. Today for sure, in the last couple of hours."

McKnight shook his head. "Slow down. What do we know for sure? What weapon from this age could do this damage?"

"A hot, very sharp sword, maybe," Tyler said. "Could you strike off a man's head and shoulder with a sword stroke and carry through to severe the arm as well? It would have to be one helluva blow. I couldn't have done it."

He chuckled. "Maybe with a light saber."

Smalls smiled.

"Not funny," McKnight said. He pulled at his lower lip. "But the evidence suggests you guys might be right. What about his clothes? Find anything in his pockets?"

"Haven't checked yet, sir," Smalls said. "We didn't want to move the body until you'd seen it. I don't know much about style, but the clothes look retro-European. Let's check his pockets. Give me a hand, Major."

Tyler and Smalls knelt by the body and checked the breast pocket and the pants' pockets.

"Nothing here," Smalls said.

"Some lint and a key in this pocket," Tyler said. "The clothes are European-looking, but not modern. They look like early twentieth century. Maybe 1920s? Definitely pre-World War II."

Time travelers from the mid-twentieth century? That can't be right.

"It looks like a Boy Scout uniform, but the colors aren't right. Okay, let's turn him over," Tyler said. "Push him toward me as I lift."

The two men lifted the body and rotated it.

"Ha!" Smalls said. He saw the weapon first. A pistol grip protruded from his waistband.

Tyler blinked. "Is that—?"

"Yes, it is," Smalls said. "It's a Luger P08 — the service weapon for Nazi officers." He shook his head. "Well, in fairness, Several European nations used the P08 as a service weapon, including the local police."

"What?" McKnight said. "Nazis? Here?"

This is like a bad B-Movie.

Smalls shrugged and pulled the weapon out. Pointing it at the ground, he ejected the rounds and examined the weapon. "It's in great condition."

"Are you a collector?" McKnight asked.

"No, but I've seen a few, fired one once, and I've read up on it."

"So, it's old, but in great shape?"

Smalls frowned as he examined the weapon.

"And?" Tyler said.

Smalls handed it to Tyler. "What do you think?"

He turned to McKnight. "I don't see any signs of wear. I think it's brand new."

Tyler nodded. "I don't see any wear or scratches. I agree… it's new."

"Well, that's just great," McKnight said. "We're here on a secret mission to 1787 and we have competition."

"I've found a wallet," Tyler said. He opened it and found a few deutschmark bills and an ID card.

"Okay, definitely German."

"Is there a date on the bills or the ID card?" McKnight asked.

"The date looks like 1935 on the ID card. This kid looks like Hitler Youth. It says something about Hitlerjugend and, under his signature, is something… 'blut und ehre'. I don't know what that means."

"Blood and Honor," McKnight said.

The two men stared at him.

"What? Did you guys sleep through history class at the Point? 'Blood and Honor' was the motto of the Hitler Youth."

Smalls chuckled. "When I was in school, I never expected to run into these guys. Who knew?"

McKnight paused for a few seconds.

"Why is he here? And why now? It can't be a coincidence."

"I can't imagine how it could be," Smalls said.

"And Hitler Youth?" McKnight said. "If it's from 1937… and I emphasize *if*… why not send a soldier? Or a platoon?"

"Is there a threat to General Washington?" Tyler said.

McKnight pointed at Tyler. "Good question, and we need the answer. Okay. Major Tyler, send a status message to Kathy and tell her we need a DNA kit and a body recovery bag right now. Ask her to send it to the last location Major Smalls jumped to."

"Yes, sir."

"And be sure to tell her the body isn't one of us."

"Yes, sir," Tyler said. He pulled out his phone, turned and walked downhill.

McKnight turned to Smalls. "Major, I'll send Cutty back up here to guard the body and keep the animals away, then you brief him and the rest of the team on the event. But don't speak to General Washington about it yet. I've gotta think about how to explain what's happened."

"Yes, sir."

McKnight shook his head. "They say no plan ever survives first contact with the real world. This is a great example."

"Yes, sir. Same stuff, different day."

"No kidding."

McKnight looked at the body again.

You were just a kid. Did they send you here to test the time engine?

McKnight turned and walked downhill.

We need a new plan.

CHAPTER TEN

Saturday, February 10th, 1787 - 12:50 PM - The Woods of Northern Virginia

The birds chirped and wind whistled through the Virginia forest.

McKnight looked up at the sky. There wasn't a cloud in sight. He stopped and looked at the surrounding woods.

Not too different from Oregon. These are great woods. I could use a head-clearing hike.

He started down the hill again and engaged his analytical mind.

Two problems — the body, and what I tell Washington. Let's table the body for now.

McKnight stopped, took a deep breath, and held it for five seconds. He repeated the process twice more. His head clearer, he started walking again.

I'm making good progress with Washington. If I tell him about this, it'll create doubt in his mind. If I don't explain it and he finds out, I'll lose his trust... But maybe not. He's a general in the army. He understands 'need to know' and strategic focus.

His thoughts continued along that path, but his emotions withdrew from it.

Do I really want to lie to one of the Founding Fathers? He shook his head. *No, I don't.*

Tyler approached him.

"I got through to Kathy, sir," he said. "She's sending the supplies as soon as she gets them together."

"Good."

McKnight glanced at the clearing as he felt the hair on his arm stand up. "I think it's coming now."

"Yes, sir."

Tyler turned and headed for the clearing.

McKnight found Cutty helping with lunch preparation.

"Lieutenant Cutty?"

"Yes, sir?"

Light flashed behind him.

The bag and test kits are here.

"Thanks for getting everything started. I need you to go relieve Major Smalls. I'm sending someone to help you bag and tag the corpse and do a DNA test. Then take both to the lab. I want Kathy and Trevor and Doctor Astalos to research and learn whatever they can, but you return here. Got it?"

"Yes, sir. Bag and tag, DNA test. Deliver to Doctor Wu. Instruct them to analyze and report. Return."

"Right. And send Major Smalls down here."

"Yes, sir," Cutty said. He pivoted and sprinted up the hill.

McKnight smiled at Cutty's enthusiasm and approached the campfire.

"Any food left?" he asked.

"Yes, sir," Lagunas said, and handed him a small plate.

He wolfed the food down and handed the plate back.

"Thank you." He rubbed his hands together. "Daze, have you eaten? Are you available to help with something?"

"Yes, on both counts, sir. What can I do?"

"Come along," he said, and motioned for her to walk with him. They turned toward Tyler, who was checking the supplies from Kathy.

"Quick update for you, Daze," McKnight said. "We found a body up the hill that doesn't belong here. I need you to help Cutty with a bag and tag, but first do a DNA test. Have you done that before?"

"Yes, sir."

"Good."

They reached Tyler in the clearing. He held up a bag containing the supplies.

"Major," McKnight said, "Daze here will assist Cutty with the work. I need you and Smalls here to discuss options."

"Yes, sir."

Tyler handed the bag to Lagunas, and she hurried up the hill. As they watched her, he saw Smalls enter the bivouac and engage Wheeler and Hatcher.

Good.

McKnight looked back over his shoulder to where Washington and Lee were reading. He found Washington staring at them. Before he could think, he smiled and gave Washington a wave. The general turned his attention back to the papers in his hands.

Sure, that put him at ease.

McKnight rubbed his eyes and looked at Tyler.

"Winnie, what are you grinning at?"

"You, sir," Tyler said. "If I may?"

"Yes, what's on your mind?"

Tyler nodded toward Washington. "You're not following your own orders, Marc. Don't put him on a pedestal. He's a retired general from the colonial army. Treat him like General Drake. He's smart. Give him the credit that's due and he'll make a quality decision."

McKnight considered this.

"Marc, don't go on my opinion. Ask Smalls what he thinks. He'll give you the straight skinny with no spin."

McKnight shook his head. "I don't have to," he said. "You got your point across."

"Yes, sir. Good."

Smalls joined them. "Okay, Colonel, I briefed the team and Cutty is on station up the hill. I saw Daze on her way up there. She's tasked with helping him?"

"Yes," McKnight said. "Okay, let's discuss. What options do we have?"

"The dead guy is from around 1937," Smalls said. "That's consistent with his uniform, the Hitler Youth thing, and considers the twenty-five-year limit on time jumps. Six times twenty-five is 150 years, the gap between 1787 and 1937. Pre-World War II Nazis have got their hands on Doctor Astalos' original technology somehow."

"Agreed," Tyler said. "But it couldn't have originated there, of course. Someone from our time period gave it to them."

"You think someone gave them a time engine?" McKnight asked.

"Maybe, but not a new one," Smalls added. "The damage to the body suggests they're using an earlier version of the technology - the time bubble. Our new technology doesn't work the same way."

"Makes sense," Tyler said. "And the damage implies they have no experience with the technology, or the kid just didn't follow instructions. Remember Wheeler's story about Hatcher and the rattlesnake? Same kind of damage."

"Right," Smalls said. "Back to my point. The first-time engines were big. The original time bubble was too small to send an engine through it, and of course you'd need another engine to do the sending."

"What are you suggesting, Major?" McKnight said.

"If they didn't have a machine, then maybe they only had the specs and blueprints."

McKnight shrugged. "That fits the evidence, and I remember when Doctor Astalos was pulling together the specs for the army. He wasn't crazy about the idea, but it was a requirement for setting up and funding the HERO project."

"Yes, sir," Smalls said. "Back to our situation. Could they have built a time engine from the specs and now are learning how to use it? That implies no previous training or user manual."

"What scares me," Tyler said, "is how did they get the specs? Most likely, someone within our government sold or gave it to someone. Who knows how many links are in that chain? How did the technology get from Doctor Astalos to 1937 Fascists?"

"Okay," McKnight said. "I think we've exhausted the known facts and are getting into conjecture. Here's the important question."

He looked back and forth between the two officers.

"Why are they here in the North Virginia mountains in 1787? Is it a coincidence? A random test of the capability? Or is it us and our mission? Who's the target? Us? General Washington? What do they have to gain by observing our mission?"

Smalls shook his head. "The chances this is a coincidence don't even register on my dial," he said. "No way. They trying to observe, maybe disrupt the mission."

"Why?" McKnight said, but it occurred to him he knew the answer.

"I think it's obvious," Tyler said. "The United States helped kick the Germans' collective asses in World War I and defeated the Axis powers on two fronts in World War II. What if the United States, for whatever reason, remained under the Articles of Confederation and never became the powerful nation we are today?"

"The perfect war," Smalls said. "Prevent the enemy from being strong enough to hurt you long before the war starts. I like it, it makes sense."

"It does," Tyler added. "Hey, here come Daze and Cutty."

The two lieutenants approached them. Cutty carried the body over his shoulder and Lagunas carried the DNA kit.

"We found something else, Colonel," Lagunas said, and held out a time beacon.

McKnight took it and examined it. Then he handed it to Tyler.

"We found it as we pulled the body into the bag," she said. "It looks like it was on a chain around his neck."

Tyler handed the beacon back to Lagunas. "Old technology, sir. This looks like the first beacon we used. You could only use it to return from time travel."

"Most likely someone is working on a learning curve," Smalls said.

"Right," Tyler said. "And it shouldn't take them long to get dangerous."

McKnight sighed. "Sure looks that way. You have your orders, Lieutenant. Get the body to the lab and come back here pronto."

"Yes, sir."

"And Daze? Give that beacon to Doctor Astalos. I want to know what their level of technology is, and what we should expect. And I want to know when and where they came from."

"Yes, sir," the two lieutenants said, and headed for the clearing.

"And don't forget the DNA sample." He called after them.

Cutty threw a thumbs-up back over his shoulder.

McKnight glanced at Washington, whose attention was on the lieutenants and their burden.

No choice now. I'll have to explain it.

He looked at Washington, who was watching him closely.

"Damn," he said. "Guess I'd better go talk to General Washington."

CHAPTER ELEVEN

<u>Saturday, February 10th, 1787 - 1:29 PM - The Woods of Northern Virginia</u>

Washington came forward to meet McKnight, a look of apprehension on his face.

"I presume something has happened that we should all be concerned with?" he said.

"Yes, sir," McKnight said. He glanced between Washington and Lee.

I need to downplay this if I can.

"Did you two get something to eat?"

"Yes," Washington said. "Your Majors Hatcher and Wheeler took good care of us." He pointed at Lagunas and Cutty. "What is amiss?"

McKnight glanced back over his shoulder in time to see the aura form around the two lieutenants and the body.

"Yes, sir, there is a problem, and we need to solve it. We found a dead body about a hundred meters up the hill from here."

Washington extended his arms to include the surrounding woods. "I daresay death strikes in these lands every day. But this one is special, isn't it? Perhaps someone who isn't supposed to be here?"

McKnight nodded.

Washington watched him and spoke again. "If the man was not important to you, then you wouldn't be carrying the body back to your time, correct?"

McKnight nodded again. "Correct."

"Did you know him?"

"No, sir, I didn't. To be clear, I'm convinced he didn't come here from my time."

Washington and Lee started, then exchanged glances.

They weren't expecting that.

"He's not from your era *or* mine. His appearance raises concerns. The evidence suggests he comes from an era 150 years from now, an era that shouldn't have the ability to travel through time as we do."

Washington still looked confused.

"It's difficult to think in terms of time travel. You're not used to thinking that way because, to you, it makes little sense. It takes time to get used to... I mean, accustomed to speculating in terms of time."

"What causes you to believe he isn't from this time?" Washington asked. "Was there something that suggested otherwise?"

"Yes, sir. The man wore a uniform from a military organization that existed during the years from 1932 to 1945. He carried papers and a weapon that tied him to that era."

"I see," Washington said. He frowned at McKnight. "What interest would a future traveler have in this time of history?" His expression changed to one of interest. "Was this man interested in your mission?"

"General Washington, I must be straightforward with you. I have no evidence that leads me to that conclusion. Nonetheless, I cannot accept his appearance here as coincidental. In fact, I can't conceive of any circumstance under which it would be coincidental."

"So, you suspect he is here to observe or interfere with your project?"

"That's a strong possibility, sir. But to be fair, I don't know if he is interested in my project, me... or you."

"Me? But why? I find this very hard to comprehend. Why would he be interested in me?"

"I have my suspicions, sir," McKnight said. "And I'll try to articulate them. Let's sit down."

They walked to the fallen tree Washington and Lee treated as their personal space for their discussions.

"Sir, I'm sure you're familiar with the idea of a fork in the road."

"I think so, Colonel, but please elaborate."

"Well, everyone comes to forks in their life's road, where the direction they take changes the rest of their life, correct?"

"Yes, I'm familiar with that concept. Pray continue, Colonel."

"General Washington, I know you have some sense of this. Your meeting in Philadelphia is a fork in the road for many people. I'm referring to the millions of people who live or will live in these states."

"I can imagine your argument, sir. Go ahead."

"Many people like me are certain you and your colleagues took the right road. It strengthened the nation and, in the future, the United States is the epitome of military might used for peace instead of conquest."

"You flatter me, sir."

McKnight shook his head. "No, sir, I don't. It's a fact. In my time, we have our problems, but our people are freer than in any other nation."

Washington nodded and waited for McKnight to finish his thought.

"To balance that, there are others who would rather the states continue with the Articles of Confederation. The fork in the road our nation takes does not exist yet, and some would rather it not exist."

"What does that mean?" Washington asked.

He's curious and listening now.

"Those leaders *could* take the same path you're considering, but they won't. Most are monarchs that would lose power if their country became a republic. So, their strength will not improve like ours has. Their other option is to prevent the United States from taking this fork in the road."

Washington nodded. "So far, sir, this has been an interesting mental exercise. Please help me understand how it applies to us now."

"Yes, sir. In the time this dead man came from, there was a great upheaval in Germany — or Prussia, as you know it. Germany's leaders had a thirst for power, and they planned to conquer Europe. It's a dark time in our world's history. They ignited what became a very large war. We called it a World War, where fighting spanned from Japan through Russia, China, all the countries of eastern Europe, France, Germany, England, Italy, Africa, and the Americas."

Washington stared at him in disbelief. "I'm not familiar with some of those countries, but it seems absurd. How could you prosecute such a widespread war, with enemies thousands of miles apart? I can't imagine it."

"Yes, sir. Even in retrospect, it's hard to imagine. Technology played a large role. In the end, the Germans and their allies were defeated and the United States helped to stop the onslaught they started."

"Tell me more about this."

"Sir, I'll be happy to, but it won't help us here and it won't answer your question. Let's save that question for later."

Washington frowned but nodded after a moment. "You're correct, of course. Please continue."

"Yes, sir. So, consider this. If the German forces had the benefit of knowing the future before they prosecuted the war…"

"You mean the outcome…?"

"Yes."

McKnight sighed. "It was horrible. Millions died in the war. And all of Europe was affected, but Germany in particular was devastated. Their economy was destroyed, and their cities reduced to rubble. All industry, vineyards, food crops… *everything* was in ruins. The war decimated their population and changed the face of Europe forever."

Washington stared at McKnight, then blinked.

"Then, does Germany no longer exist in your time?"

"It does, but its place in the world has diminished. But that's not what matters now. After the war, decades passed before Germany recovered."

"I find this amazing," Washington said. "Germany was on its knees. Was it not conquered? Was it so ruined that no country wanted it?"

"Oh, I'm sure several countries wanted it, but both sides had experienced six years of constant, total warfare. Enemies surrounded Germany at the end, but maybe none of the countries had the stomach to fight another battle over meager spoils."

"I can understand that," Washington said. "Our fight against the British lasted six years, and it was all I could bear. I understand the sentiment. I would be reluctant to repeat the experience."

"The reasons they stopped fighting were complex, but let's return to my line of reasoning. If Germany had known the result of the war beforehand, then—"

"They wouldn't start the fight. They would reexamine their plans and try another way of accomplishing their goals. That would seem prudent."

"That's one possibility."

"What else might they try?" the old soldier asked.

McKnight hesitated.

I don't know enough history to guess. We need a real historian.

"We need someone with more history expertise to interpret this," McKnight said. "Sir, I'll share my opinion, but I must warn you I'm not an expert on that time in history."

"A wise man knows what he does not know and admits it."

"I'm sure that's true, General. I just want to impress upon you that my insight into this is limited and I'm raising conjecture and little else."

Washington grunted. "Point taken, Colonel McKnight." He stood and stared at a mountain three miles away. Barren trees and scattered snow covered its slopes. He looked up at the sky. The clouds had increased during the day and the temperature dropped when they obscured the sun.

"Will, it looks like snow, doesn't it?" Washington said.

"Yes, sir," Lee replied. "We'd better get indoors or find some shelter. It's going to get mighty cold here tonight."

"I agree. We should plan for a chilly night."

He turned back toward McKnight.

"Colonel, I'd still like to hear your thoughts. I accept your premise that it is your opinion."

"Thank you, General. I appreciate that. I didn't want to influence your decisions with my uneducated opinion."

"Good. Please continue. Tell me what concerns you."

"It's just that…" McKnight said, and paused only for an instant.

Say what you know. Don't speculate on what you don't know.

"Well, I *do* appreciate one thing about the people who instigated the war. They were ruthless, and they wouldn't give up their plans. They would… stack the deck, if you get my meaning."

"I do."

McKnight continued. "The United States was strong. The war might have ended differently if the United States had not entered the fight against Germany and her allies."

"You imply Germany might have won the war but for the efforts of the United States?"

"Yes, sir, I do."

"I'm unpracticed in considering what might have been. I've never thought about it. It's hard to imagine the consequences of changing history, if that's even possible."

"Oh, it is, sir. Believe me, it is."

Washington straightened and looked McKnight in the eye.

"You've done this?"

"Yes, sir."

Washington looked confused.

"But I thought you considered changing history a bad thing? Why would you do it if you knew how dangerous it is?"

McKnight shook his head. "Ah, let me be more specific, General Washington. The changes I have made, with one exception, pushed history back onto its original course after others changed it."

"I see. With one exception? Curious. I'd like to hear about that."

"It's a private matter, sir."

Washington sat back on the log next to Lee, who was watching McKnight. The general rocked back and forth for a few seconds, then looked up at McKnight.

"You can learn a lot about a man if you study the times he violated orders."

McKnight shook his head. "No, sir, I didn't violate orders, sir. I followed orders. But I considered them wrong."

"Tell me," Washington ordered.

McKnight faced the father of his country. "Yes, sir." He sat next to him on the log.

"Our mission was to correct a history change we couldn't prevent. It was necessary to kill a man to do it, and we knew when and where he was going to be. I assure you, sir, he deserved death many times over for his crimes. We could kill him, and that was the plan."

McKnight's posture sagged as he spoke.

"Coincidentally, it gave us an opportunity to save a life that was otherwise lost. My leadership judged it would be good to salvage something out of the mission. To do some good."

Washington didn't blink. "What did you do?" he asked.

McKnight paused before he spoke, and his voice was husky.

"I turned my father's assassination into a failed assassination attempt."

Lee and Washington said nothing. The wind picked up and the dead leaves in the trees rattled and clattered overhead.

"Is he still alive?" Lee asked.

"No, sir," McKnight said. "He died of an illness later. Our history change gave me more memories, but I never got to experience him as an adult."

Washington sighed.

"I am sorry, Colonel, for compelling you to relive a sad memory. Can you forgive me?"

"There's nothing to forgive, sir." McKnight stood and brushed at his uniform. "So let me finish my opinion for you, sir. What occurred to me is that your efforts in the next few months will put the United States on a firmer foundation. One that will make her strong and determined to fight tyranny."

"Isn't that a good thing?"

"Of course it is, sir. But in Germany, one hundred-fifty years from now, these tyrants won't appreciate what you've done. If they can stop the work you are doing, Germany might win that war."

Washington hesitated before responding. "That is not what I was expecting."

"Yes, sir. It takes practice to think like we — my team and I — must every day."

Washington looked at Lee, then back at McKnight.

"Are our lives in danger?"

"If I must guess, I'd say yes, sir. Killing you and anyone who takes your place would be a simple act with potential to keep the United States out of that war."

Washington scanned the sky again.

"Will and I need to move on. With the weather threatening, we'll need shelter. Colonel, I want to digest this overnight. There is much to consider. Can I give you my answer in the morning?"

Not what I wanted to hear, but I can't make him help us.

"Of course, sir. Where are you going tonight?"

"There's a settlement about four miles down the hill, just on the other side of the Shenandoah River. A family of my acquaintance owns a farm on this side. They will take us in for the night."

"Very good, sir," McKnight said.

"Thank you, Colonel McKnight, for a stimulating conversation, though I'm troubled by the potential outcomes."

He turned to Lee. "Will, start packing for the hike down the hill."

"I understand how you feel, General."

Washington turned back to McKnight. "Colonel, I look forward to talking to you tomorrow."

"Yes, sir. Me, too."

Don't be dismissed so easily. He needs to understand the danger.

"General, I will assign two officers to shadow you and make sure you and Mr. Lee are safe tonight. The rest of us will go back to our time and return here tomorrow morning. My people will communicate your location to me."

"I'm sure protection will be unnecessary, Colonel."

McKnight smiled at Washington. "You may be correct, sir, but it's a prudent precaution and simple to implement."

"Do you suppose we are in danger tonight? How would any... traveler... find us here?"

"You saw our technology, sir. We found you. They have a great deal of technology themselves. Don't underestimate them. They're resourceful and dedicated to their cause. If there's a way to track you down, they'll find it. I don't want to see you hurt or killed, sir."

"That would end your mission as well, wouldn't it?"

"Sir?"

"Hmmpf," Washington said. "Forgive me, Colonel. I owe you an apology. You've done nothing to make me suspect you aren't concerned about my well-being. But, you understand, I haven't lived this long without a healthy respect for the baser motives of humanity."

Crafty old guy.

"Yes, sir, I understand, and I will instruct them to stay out of sight unless you need them. I'll communicate with them and meet you wherever you are. May I suggest ten o'clock tomorrow morning?"

"Yes, that is acceptable... and, Colonel McKnight, I respect what you are attempting to do, and I appreciate your courtesy. It crossed my mind that, given your technology, you could have taken me without asking permission, but you didn't. Why?"

McKnight hesitated for a moment.

"I understand your curiosity about that, sir. There are people in my time who suggested that strategy. It made little sense to me and my commanding officer. The chances of you being able to influence the citizens of the future are slim, but they would be worse if you were there against your will. No, sir, we have a better chance of success if you understand and see the logic of what we're asking you to do and approach the problem voluntarily."

Washington nodded. "I see."

He stepped toward McKnight and extended his hand. "I look forward to seeing you tomorrow, whatever my decision."

"The feeling is mutual, sir," McKnight said. "Whatever you decide, we will respect your decision. And it has been my honor to meet you, sir, and I hope we get to work together to save our nation."

"It is my honor as well. We'll talk tomorrow."

He looked back at Lee, who was packing their gear and provisions. Lee glanced at the clouds overhead.

Washington turned back to McKnight.

"Now I must take my leave of you. I want to assist Will and find shelter before the snow hits."

"Yes, sir. And we must break camp and clean up the area. Until tomorrow at ten, sir?"

Washington nodded. "Yes. Hurry on then, and let us move toward our night's rest."

McKnight came to attention and saluted Washington. Then he turned on his heel and walked back to the Ranger bivouac.

CHAPTER TWELVE

Saturday, February 10th, 1787 - 1:40 PM - The Woods of Northern Virginia

As McKnight approached the Ranger camp. Smalls and Tyler hurried to him while Hatcher and Wheeler continued to police the bivouac.

"Well, sir?" Tyler said. "What's the verdict?"

Smalls couldn't conceal a look of eagerness.

"The jury's still out, Major. We're meeting again in the morning. He wants to sleep on the idea."

"That doesn't sound good," Smalls said.

"No, but it's all we've got. I think he was pretty close to agreeing before we found the body. That was a definite downer. I had to explain why evil people from a different era want him dead for doing something he hasn't done yet."

Tyler laughed, and McKnight glared at him.

"No offense intended, sir, but I'd have loved to hear that discussion."

McKnight shrugged. "None taken. If it sounds lame to you guys, how do you suppose it sounds to Washington?"

Tyler and Smalls glanced at each other.

"Yes, sir," Smalls said. "I see what you mean. Any orders, sir?"

McKnight sighed. "I need to get back to 2037 and give a poor results status report."

"Sorry, sir," Tyler said.

"It is what it is."

He pointed at Smalls. "When I get to the lab, I'm going to send Cutty and Lagunas back here. I want them to shadow the General tonight and make sure nothing happens to him. They're tired, but they scouted this area for weeks and know it better than any of us. I'll be back at ten hundred tomorrow to meet with him. Make sure they protect him, but try to keep out of sight so he doesn't feel like they're spying on him."

"Yes, sir."

"Major Tyler, I want you, Hatcher, and Wheeler to make it look like our camp never existed. Pack up everything and police the area. Don't leave any technology or evidence of it behind, understood?"

"Yes, sir. Shall we dig the M4 slugs out of the tree where Lieutenant Cutty so carelessly discarded them?"

Despite himself, McKnight couldn't suppress a smile. "I think those will be okay where he left them, Major Tyler. Just wrap up everything and make it appear we were never here. Then bring the gear back to 2037 with you. Clear?"

"Yes, sir."

McKnight shook his head. "General Drake and Senator Lodge are *not* going to be happy."

"Yes, sir," Smalls said. "We'll be right behind you as soon as we finish up here."

"Good," McKnight said. He turned, walked to the clearing, and pressed the return button on his beacon twice.

****

Saturday, February 10th, 1937 - 7:40 PM - The German Chancellery - Berlin, Germany

Colonel Hans Bittner sat in the waiting room outside the office of Reichsführer Henrich Himmler. He finished his coffee and set the china cup back in its saucer on the side table.

These status meetings with Himmler were always unsettling. There were rumors that officers who displeased Himmler were demoted and disgraced.

Bittner had no evidence that the rumors were true.

But I've never given him bad news.

The comely blonde woman approached him.

What was her name?

"The Reichsführer is ready to see you, Colonel."

Bittner jumped to his feet and picked up his briefcase.

"Thank you," he said, then silently cursed himself for the tremor in his voice.

He followed her to the huge double doors of Himmler's office.

Walk confidently. Head high. Look him in the eye. Think before you speak.

Bittner approached Himmler's desk, snapped to attention, and presented the Nazi salute.

Himmler sat still, looking at papers with a pen in his hand. He left Bittner standing there for ten seconds before acknowledging his presence with a casual salute.

Bittner returned to his attention stance.

Himmler looked up at him and said, "Sit down, Colonel."

Bittner felt a surge of panic as he walked between the two chairs.

Which one should I choose? Fool! It's not important.

He chose the left chair, set his briefcase next to it, and sat.

Himmler laid his pen on the desk and looked at Bittner.

"So, tell me," he said. "What intelligence was brought back from 1787 in America?"

Bittner's voice caught in his throat. He cleared it and spoke. "The traveler didn't return with a report, Herr Reichsführer."

Himmler stared for a moment without blinking.

"Why not?" he asked.

"He didn't return at all, sir."

Himmler didn't respond.

Bittner squirmed. The absence of eye-blinking was disconcerting.

Say something!

"Could it be because only part of him traveled to the eighteenth century?"

He knows. I should have guessed.

"Yes, sir," he said, struggling to keep his voice even. "He was killed by the time engine, sir."

Himmler nodded. "Why did we not expect this possibility?"

"Sir, the engine creates a time bubble that is less than two meters in diameter. He was large for his age. We were not told about this engine aspect. We did not know of any danger to large test subjects."

Be quiet! Don't babble!

"And why were you not told?" Himmler stared at him.

"Herr Reichsführer, we built the engine from the designs provided, but there were only drawings and measurements. There were no operating instructions with it."

When Himmler did not respond, Bittner added, "His family are good party members, and it will grieve them to learn of his death."

Himmler shook his head and dismissed Bittner's comment with a wave.

"Do you now understand the issue? Can you overcome it?"

"Yes, sir."

"Then try again. The future of the Reich depends on your ability to accomplish your mission."

"Yes, sir."

Himmler glared at Bittner. "Let me remind you, Colonel. I want you to bring this Washington person to me or kill him if you cannot. But I would much prefer that you bring him to me. Do you understand me, Colonel?"

"Yes, my Reichsführer."

"Good."

Himmler smiled without warmth. "Don't come back with more failure. I'm only interested in seeing you if you have something valuable to report. You are dismissed."

Bittner jumped to his feet and saluted. "Sieg heil!"

Himmler threw a small salute back, mumbled "Sieg heil", and returned to the papers on his desk.

Bittner picked up his briefcase and strode out of Himmler's private office, passed the receptionist, and left the executive offices. He entered the fire stairwell, leaned against the wall, and hyperventilated.

I never want to experience that again.

He pushed his fear away and calmed himself enough to think.

Next time I come here, I'll have results that make him happy.

CHAPTER THIRTEEN

Tuesday, February 10th, 2037 - 1:50 PM EST - HERO Team Lab, Telegraph Road, Alexandria, Virginia

Stars sped past McKnight's eyes and gave way to the HERO Team Lab.

"Welcome back, Colonel," Kathy said.

"Ditto," Trevor said. "General Drake and Senator Lodge are waiting for you in the big conference room."

"Thanks. Tell them I'll be there in ten minutes. In the meantime, can you turn on the block for this site? I mean, so no one can jump here without our permission? We don't want any uninvited guests."

"Yes, sir," Trevor said. "It should always be on, but I'll confirm. I'm on it."

"Good. Please text me when the rest of the team returns."

"You got it, Colonel."

Cutty and Lagunas stood in the break area, checking their equipment.

When they saw him approaching, they dropped everything and came to attention.

"As you were," McKnight said.

"Sir, we turned the body over to Kathy and Trevor. She called Doctor Astalos, and he is on his way here."

"Good. Now, I need you to go back to 1787 and stick with General Washington. I'm meeting with him tomorrow at ten, and your job is to shadow and protect him until I get there. Stay out of sight if you can but be ready to interfere if anyone comes after him."

"Understood, sir," Cutty said. "Are we expecting any trouble? Should we carry more than the standard firepower?"

McKnight paused.

I didn't think of that. It's a good idea.

"Yes, good idea, Lieutenant. And take some cold weather gear. You'll be out in the wild and they're expecting snow."

"Wonderful," Lagunas said. "Are we expecting more Nazis… for lack of an adequate word, sir?"

"I'm not expecting anyone. Better to be safe than sorry. Keep your eye out for any threat to General Washington. You know how important it is for him to be safe and at that meeting in Philadelphia in three months."

"Yes, sir," she said. "One more question."

She looked at Cutty, who nodded back at her.

"We were talking earlier, sir. We're not allowed to change history, right? What if we run into someone who's targeting General Washington? I can't imagine that we would let that happen."

McKnight considered her question.

She's really looking for guidance.

"You're right, Lieutenant. There are two scenarios that might happen. One scenario is like what happened when we found the general. Those were local time people. Interfere there only as a last resort, but don't allow anything to happen to General Washington."

"Yes, sir. And the other circumstance?"

"All bets are off if you come up against other time travelers. They are there to disrupt history and our job is to preserve it. Consider yourselves in a combat situation and don't allow these people near the general. I authorize lethal force at your discretion as needed."

"Yes, sir," they replied in unison.

"Carry on," McKnight said.

The two lieutenants turned and sped off in different directions. Lagunas went to arrange their time travel and Cutty went to the armory.

McKnight exited the lab and strode down the hallway to the conference room. As he entered, he saw General Drake and Senator

Lodge sitting at the conference table, an empty chair between them and coffee cups in front of them.

McKnight approached Drake, came to attention, and saluted.

Drake returned the salute and said, "As you were, Colonel. Help yourself to coffee and come join us."

"Thank you, sir," he said, and walked to the coffee service, poured his coffee, and returned to sit between the two men.

"What's your report, Colonel?" Lodge said. "Did Washington come back with you?"

"No, sir. Not yet."

Lodge opened his mouth to say more, but Drake held up his hand.

"James, let the man catch his breath."

Drake turned to McKnight. "No casualties, Marc? Is the team okay?"

"Yes, sir. Thanks for asking. I've dispatched Cutty and Lagunas to shadow General Washington overnight, just in case. I presume they briefed you on the body Cutty found?"

"Yes," Drake said. "That's troubling. Let's address that first."

"Yes, sir."

"Trevor and Kathy pulled configuration data off the beacon you found and will have the boy's origin soon. There are two action items here. We need to find them and put them out of commission. And we need to know how they got the technology and if anybody else out there has it."

"I agree," McKnight said. "I'll enlist Trevor and Kathy to help. Cold case investigation is Trevor's thing, and you know he's good at it."

"You read my mind. Who else?"

McKnight nodded. "Wheeler and Hatcher, sir. They have experience with working out cross-time activity streams, and I'm sure they'll want the job."

"Umm-Hmm." Drake pulled at his chin. "This is number one priority. We can't have pre-World War II Nazis traveling through time. That's a scary thought."

"Yes, sir. So, the General Washington project is…?"

"Still on," Drake said. "We might have to speed up our plan by bringing him forward in time just to keep him alive. Even if he doesn't want to come."

"I hope you won't order me to do that, sir. I have a good rapport with him, but grabbing him without permission will destroy all credibility I have."

"I agree," Drake said, "but there's been a recent development you don't know about."

"And what's that, sir?"

"The standoff in St. Louis got hot today. Two radical right-wing extremists crossed the Mississippi from St. Louis and killed a couple of enlisted men who challenged them. They escaped across the river, and the Army is screaming for permission to go get them, or for the opposition to turn them over. The opposition is condemning the extremists' actions, but they're not giving them up."

"That doesn't sound good."

"No, it's not. It's only a matter of time before real warfare starts. When that happens, we'll have an honest-to-God civil war on our hands."

We're running out of time.

"How long do you think we have?" McKnight asked.

"No more than a month," Drake said. "Maybe as little as two weeks." He turned to Lodge. "Do you agree, James?"

"For the most part, yes," Lodge said. His voice rasped, then broke into a deep cough.

McKnight read the look on the Senator's face.

He's in pain.

Lodge recovered from the cough and spoke. "So, what's the real holdup with Washington? Is he afraid? Did finding that Nazi body upset him?"

Drake pointed at Lodge. "Wouldn't *you* be upset by that?"

Lodge settled back in his chair. "Yes, I guess so. So, what do you think, Colonel McKnight? Will he help us?"

McKnight considered the question.

"I can see it from his point of view, sir. We spring this 'from the future' thing on him, which is a lot to take in, all by itself. Then he finds out another guy came from the future to stop him, maybe with deadly force."

Drake nodded, but Lodge looked unconvinced.

"See it from his side, Senator," McKnight said. "People are popping in out of thin air and maybe they're friendly, maybe they're not. Then we want him to jump with us into an unknown future? How would you feel?"

Lodge's expression didn't change.

Lodge doesn't get it. Or he doesn't care.

McKnight drained the rest of his coffee. His phone chirped, and he read the text. "The team is back," he said.

He stood and walked to the coffee service. "If I were him, I'd look for a defensive position on my turf and defend myself from there."

He poured a fresh cup of coffee.

"Don't you see? History tells us that Washington's natural inclination is to control everything around him. There are way too many variables here he can't control... No, sir, the more I think about it, the more positive I am he'll decide to stay put. I'd give you three-to-one odds that he'll decline."

"If that's the case, then why not change the narrative?" Lodge said. "Tell him you checked it out and the Nazi guy wasn't there for him at all. It's all good. C'mon to the future and help us out."

"You mean lie to him to get him to come along?"

"I wouldn't be so blunt, Colonel, but... okay, why not?"

Because I'm a terrible liar.

"Because a lie to get him here under false pretenses will come back to bite us in the ass, sir. Besides, you haven't met him yet. I have. He's a shrewd judge of people and suspicious by nature. He'll know a lie when he hears one. Besides, given what he already knows or has imagined, lying to him will make everything worse."

Lodge's cell phone pinged, and he pulled it out to read the text. He tapped out a brief response, then stood, gathered his notes, and stuffed them into his briefcase.

"I hope you know what you're doing, Colonel McKnight," he said. "The nation depends on you to get this done, no matter what you have to do."

Lodge turned to Drake. "Congress is going to pass a resolution that will give the President more power and I need to be there. Good luck to you both."

A sudden wracking cough took Lodge again. This spasm lasted longer than the first one.

"Are you okay, James?" Drake said. "Can I get you something?"

"No, I'm fine," Lodge said, then left the conference room without another word.

Neither Drake nor McKnight spoke, waiting to be sure Lodge was out of earshot.

Drake shook his head. "That man is not well. There's something bad going on there."

"Yes, sir. But he'd rather die than have us know it."

Drake nodded. "I agree. For what it's worth, Marc, I think you're doing it the right way. If General Washington doesn't come willingly, he won't be any help at all."

"Thank you, sir. I hope I'm right, but I'm not so confident that I can pull this off. He's not afraid... He sees a battle coming at him and being on his own turf is the only thing he can control."

Drake nodded. "I see," he said. "Would it be helpful for me to return to 1787 with you and talk to him, retired general to retired general?"

"Are you sure, sir?"

"Sure, why not? I mean, if I can help."

Ha! He wants to go.

"I'm sure you'd be an asset, sir. I'll bet you can say some things from experience he can relate to."

Drake smiled. "You sold me, Marc. I'll come along and do whatever I can."

"That's excellent, sir. I appreciate your help."

"Good. Go talk to your team to see if we have anything else to deal with."

"Yes, sir," McKnight said. He stood, snapped to attention, and saluted Drake. Then he left the room and headed for the lab.

Better. With General Drake with us, the odds of Washington coming back with us just got better.

CHAPTER FOURTEEN

Tuesday, February 10th, 1787 - 2:00 PM EST - The Woods of Northern Virginia

Cutty and Lagunas landed at the 1787 campsite. Smalls and Wheeler were still there, packing up and hiding traces of the bivouac.

"General Washington was in a hurry," Smalls said. "He and Mr. Lee left about ten minutes ago. I didn't want them traveling without protection, so I sent Hatcher with them. Did you bring comms? I'm sure you'll need them."

"We have our PNRs," Cutty said.

Smalls nodded and looked at the sky. "It's gonna be a dark night… and wet. You have your night goggles? You'll need them."

"Yes, sir!"

"Good. Tell Hatcher to get back here on the double."

"Yes, sir!"

They turned and double-timed it up the hillside. As they entered the trail, they looked uphill and saw the three a quarter mile ahead. Washington's party crested the ridge and started down the far side of the mountain.

"Great," Lagunas said. "Another opportunity to run up a hill."

Cutty laughed.

That's probably the easiest part of this mission.

He glanced at Lagunas and met her eyes.

"Shut up, Eddy."

Cutty laughed again.

The slope wasn't as steep as he expected. Within five minutes, they caught up with the others.

"Captain Hatcher," Cutty said, "We're here to relieve you. Major Smalls wants you to double-time back."

"Is there any other way?" she said. "He's ready to go home."

"Hooah," Lagunas said, as Hatcher dug in and ran back over the crest of the hill.

Washington turned to them. "Are you my escorts, then?"

"Yes, sir," Lagunas said. "We'll be moving to your flanks, but we'll keep watch over you. If you run across any problems, sing out."

Washington looked puzzled.

"Sorry, sir," she said. "I meant to say you should yell or call out if you need us."

He frowned, then nodded. With Will Lee, he turned and continued down the trail to the valley.

"Well," she said, "let's get going."

"Wait, Daze. Hear that?"

A light clatter came from the treetops, and then from the surrounding brush and leaves on the ground.

"What? Rain?" she said.

"No, worse… sleet. Button up. The snow will come next."

"Roger that."

They set their weapons on the ground, pulled out their rain gear, and put it on.

Cutty picked up his weapon. "Uphill or downhill, Daze?"

"I don't care," she said. "You pick."

"Not fair. I'll give you the downhill on the right flank if you let me."

"I don't care."

"Okay," Cutty said. "I'll take the downhill."

"Too bad it's not summer," she said. "We could shadow closer if the leaves were on the trees."

Cutty snickered. "If a frog didn't jump…"

"Yeah, yeah… He wouldn't bump his ass. Let's roll."

"I'm right flank, downhill."

"Asshole."

"Yes, ma'am. See you soon."

He jumped off the path and half-walked, half-slid down the hill to the trees below. He'd have a steep incline to traverse if the general needed him.

The sound of sleet landing on the brush and trees crowded out all other nature sounds. It was sleeting harder now, and Cutty was thankful for his rain gear.

I need to keep watching the general. I won't be able to hear him over this crap.

He looked back up the hill to see Lagunas climb off the path on the left flank and make her way to the trees above.

This won't be easy... Washington's walking a well-traveled path and we're tramping through the stumps, fallen trees, and brush. And trying to be quiet.

He looked up.

Not to mention the sleet. I hope it changes to snow. At least that'll muffle sounds.

It *was* hard work, struggling through the woods. Once, he lost sight of Washington and sprinted as best he could until he could see him again.

After three hours, he saw signs of civilization.

The sun slid behind the westward mountains, casting twilight over the woodlands. The wind picked up, and the trees groaned as it pushed them back and forth.

And the sleet turned to snow, and visibility declined.

The path turned downward into a valley. Cutty heard a stream babbling nearby, somewhere up ahead. Through the trees, he made out a few lines of plowed field in the valley below, partially hidden by the accumulating snow. He smelled a wood fire.

Well, there's somebody's place ahead.

In another five minutes, Cutty came out of the woods onto the valley plain.

The daylight was waning fast, and the snow hurt visibility.

A farm.

There was a fence before him, a snowy field, a fence on the far side, and a babbling river beyond it. On the other side of the river, there was more pasture, but it was unfenced. It occurred to Cutty that the valley was an ancient flood plain for the tiny river.

We must be close.

He looked for Washington through the falling snow. The path they were following should meet the plain to his left. Over the wind, he heard hushed voices. He trotted to where he expected the trail to be. When he found it, he guessed it was forty meters from where he came out of the woods. He peered into the blowing snow, looking for the general and his butler.

He slipped on his goggles and dialed them to night vision.

Visibility was worse.

Cutty chuckled to himself.

Here I am, using night vision in the snow.

He switched his goggles to thermal imaging, and there they were.

The path at his feet turned west here, away from him. Washington and Will Lee were thirty meters further along the trail, which now looked more like a road. He followed them.

The road hugged the tree line at the bottom of the hill. Squinting, Cutty could make out a hedge coming from the trees on the left and paralleling the road for a distance.

Cutty removed his googles. Past the hedge, there was a corral, and the road curved to the right. His eyes followed the curve until, fifty meters away, a bridge leaped across the stream.

He replaced his googles and scanned the hill for Lagunas but didn't see her.

Cutty looked back at Washington. The general stood by the hedge and gazed into the woods. Lagunas stepped out of the trees and spoke with him and Will Lee. He took a last three-sixty turn and trotted toward them. Beyond them, he could make out the heat signature of a working chimney.

Must be a house there.

Before he reached them, Lagunas nodded to the others, and Washington and Lee walked backwards down the road toward the house. They waved in his direction, then turned and strode away from him. Lagunas stood still, waiting for Cutty.

When he reached her, he slipped off his goggles.

She stood with her arms crossed and tapped her foot. "Slowpoke," she said.

"Yeah, yeah."

Cutty leaned over and rested his palms on his knees as he caught his breath. He looked down the road in time to see Washington turn left and disappear behind the hedge. He straightened and turned to Lagunas.

"Lovely weather," he said. "What's the plan?"

"It's a wonderful plan." She took his arm and pointed up the forested hill behind the farmhouse. "See those trees?"

"Are you kidding?"

Lagunas giggled. "You'll like this, I promise. We get to sleep in some magnificent trees. Check this out."

She beckoned him forward.

Cutty rolled his eyes and followed her.

Lagunas led him to where the hedge met the woods at the bottom of the hill. Together, they slipped around the hedge.

Before them was a low bunkhouse. Beyond that was a shed, and then the house. It was a two-story wooden house built up against the mountain so the second-story windows were at ground level on the rising hill. There were hundreds of trees on the hillside, but two immense oak trees dominated the scene, bracketing the back corners of the house.

Lagunas grinned at him.

"See, Eddy? We sleep in those two trees, with a perfect view of the valley. Nobody can get near this place without us knowing about it."

"Except for the snow…"

Lagunas looked up at the sky. "I think it's slacking up. Don't you?"

Cutty looked up. "Maybe. Probably." He glanced around. "About three inches on the ground." He shook his head. "Makes it easier to track us."

"Or vice versa," she said. "We just need to stay alert. Let's go make our tree houses."

"Gimme a barracks rack any time over a tree, Daze… but I get it. It's a great lookout position. What about General Washington? Where will he be?"

"He told me he's stayed here before on two occasions. The farm belongs to Able and Mattie Joyner. They're in their late thirties. They have two boys and a girl, ages eight to ten. Both times before, the general stayed upstairs in the left back bedroom. He said he would come out after dinner to confirm his location."

"Sounds good. It's getting dark. Let's get up in those trees before it gets too dark to get the lay of the land."

"Hooah," Lagunas said.

CHAPTER FIFTEEN

Tuesday, February 10th, 1787 - 10:15 PM EST - The Woods of Northern Virginia

Colonel Hans Bittner landed in the year 1787 and fell backwards. He rolled to his feet and moved away from the landing zone. Lieutenant Weber, the platoon leader, arrived a moment later. Bittner beckoned him forward.

"You must move," he said. "If you stay there, you will be killed by the time bubble when the next man travels. Take up station here and keep the men moving out of the way as they arrive. When all have arrived, bring the squad leaders to me."

"Ja, wohl," Weber said, and turned to face the landing zone.

Bittner brushed snow off his uniform and walked to the mountain trail. Snowflakes were spinning around him. The snow was light, but enough accumulated to cover his boots to the ankles.

Somewhere near here we should find the body of the boy.

He looked around, but he couldn't see in the low light.

An uproar from the landing zone drove thoughts of the dead youth from his mind. A trooper didn't move before the next traveler arrived.

Bittner shook his head.

Idiots!

After his meeting with Himmler earlier, he left nothing to chance. He planned to travel with a squad before, but now he opted for a platoon. With a platoon came four machine gun teams and a mortar.

Forty-six men are more than I need, but I won't return without a victory. I will bring back this General Washington, or proof of his death.

It was darker now. He realized the time travel bubble was no longer appearing.

Ach, we are here now.

At first, the darkness unsettled him, but as his eyes adjusted, he could make out shapes. Weber and his four squad leaders joined him. Bittner and the five men moved away from the rest of the platoon. He sat on a fallen tree next to the trail and motioned Weber and the squad leaders to join him. The men approached him and knelt.

"Losses?" he asked.

Weber pointed to one of the squad leaders.

"Sergeant Schäfer, sir. One of my riflemen was killed when he didn't move out of the landing area. The time travel made him ill, and he was vomiting. Lieutenant Weber told him to move, but he ignored the order."

"Understood," Bittner said. "And the other casualty?"

Another leader spoke. "Sergeant Hoffmann, sir. I have no excuse for it, but one of my riflemen refused to get on the time engine platform. He didn't travel with us. My apologies, sir."

"I am surprised, Hoffmann," Bittner said. "How do you explain this?"

"I have no excuse or explanation, sir. If you will allow me, I shall return and bring the coward back with me."

He's eager to please and embarrassed by his rifleman's cowardice.

"No, Sergeant. I think we can do without him. But please reprimand him when we return."

"Yes, sir!" Hoffman said.

Bittner squinted to make out the faces of the squad leaders. The last two remained silent.

Bittner pointed at one of them.

"Who are you?" he said.

"Sergeant Olmann, sir," the man said. "I command third squad."

Olmann glanced at the last squad leader, and Bittner pointed at him.

"I am Sergeant Koch, sir," he said. "I command fourth squad."

Bittner nodded.

"Very good," he said. He glanced at the troops.

"Equipment? Do we have everything?"

Eager nods from the squad leaders.

"Good. We will proceed. Can we determine which way Washington went from here?"

"Sergeant Koch is our best tracker, sir," Weber said. "Koch, what can you tell from the trail?"

Koch walked a few yards up the trail and knelt. He switched on a small flashlight and trained it on the ground. After a moment, he returned to Bittner.

"Colonel, I believe they have marched to the west... up this trail and over the mountain. I found many signs of travel here, but most recently, at least four people and two horses walked up the trail. The snow hid most of their tracks in the last few hours." He looked up at the sky. "We are fortunate to have any sign."

"What makes you believe it was Washington?"

"Sir, two travelers were wearing boots. The rest leave an unusual footprint. It has a pattern, not unlike climbing shoes. I don't know if any footwear from 1787 has a patterned sole..."

"And your conclusion?"

"Two of them are not from this time period, sir. We're not the only time travelers here."

Bittner considered the logic of the man's report.

"Very good, Koch," he said. "We will travel west. Weber, deploy your platoon across the trail and on both sides. Spread out and report anything unusual. Endeavor not to be seen by people of this time period... for now. We will engage them as we must."

Bittner walked on the trail. Behind him, the squads deployed to both sides of the road.

After ten minutes, they crested the mountain and started a long descent into the next valley.

At two in the morning, they reached the valley plain. Bittner stopped and ordered Weber to recall the platoon and gather the squad leaders. He watched in silence as the platoon gathered by the road behind him. When the squad leaders gathered, he whispered to Weber.

"Send out scouts to learn what houses or towns are nearby. Tell them to stay within 200 meters of here. Report back in twenty minutes. Tell the men to make no noise and show no light, not even a cigarette."

"Yes, sir," Weber said, and dashed off to the platoon to carry out the orders.

Bittner found a stone to sit on and massaged his knees and calves.

The scouts returned and met with Weber, who brought them to Bittner.

"I'll give the report, Colonel," Weber said, "but the men will correct me if I missed anything."

He knelt before Bittner and the others followed his action.

"Sir, there's a farmhouse on the left about 150 meters down the road," Weber said. "Someone is awake... we can see lights on the ground floor." Weber gestured with his arm. "This road goes past the farmhouse, then curves to the right and crosses the river. A large hedge hides the road from the farmhouse until you reach the walkway. Behind the hedge is a low-lying building, and a shed. Past the hedge and the farmhouse — where the path turns right — there is a corral on the left side and a large barn between it and the hillside. Oh, and..." He smiled. "There are two horses in the corral. Both of them have an 'MV' mark on its flank."

"What does this 'MV' signify?" Bittner asked.

"I have studied American history, sir. Mount Vernon is the traditional home of General Washington. The 'MV' brand on the horses—"

"Yes, yes, I understand. Continue your report."

"That is the end of my report, sir." He looked at the three scouts. "Have I omitted anything?"

The scouts shook their heads.

Weber nodded back and said, "Thank you. You are dismissed."

The scouts scurried away to join the platoon.

To Bittner, he said, "What are your orders, sir?"

Bittner pulled at his lower lip and stared out into the night.

"There were lights on in the house?" he said. "You and I will approach the front entrance and ask how far it is to the next town. While we are there, the platoon will deploy to cut off escape and we will have him, correct?"

"Yes, sir."

"Thank you, Lieutenant Weber. And look… the snow has stopped. Let us see to the deployment of the platoon."

CHAPTER SIXTEEN

Tuesday, February 11th, 1787 - 2:26 AM EST - The Woods of Northern Virginia

Lagunas took the first watch. After sitting in the gigantic oak for hours, her ears learned the sounds of nature around her. Anything unusual would stand out.

It was quiet. She felt herself getting stiff from the cold and the lack of movement.

Looking left, she saw Cutty where he slept in the opposite tree.

Out cold. Thank God he doesn't snore.

Lagunas was glad for the trees. Her position gave her an unparalleled view of the farm and the valley beyond it. Now that the snow had stopped, she could see better. The cloud cover lessened, allowing moonlight to reflect off the snow and improve visibility.

She looked at her watch. She allowed Cutty to sleep longer than agreed.

Time to wake him.

Alarm bells in her head started ringing.

There's movement along the road.

"Cutty," she whispered into her PNR unit. She looked across to the other tree. She found his face among the leaves. He was awake and listening to her.

"I hear sounds on the road. We have company."

"Roger that," he said. "There are men on the road. At least seven or eight, walking in formation."

"Yup," Lagunas said. "More Nazis, you think?"

"Dunno. Maybe. Suppressors on."

"Roger."

She screwed the suppressor onto the end of her M4A1.

She saw eight men come from behind the hedge toward the front door.

"Cutty, we can't cover the front porch from here. You watch the field and the left side. I'm scouting to the right to cover the door and the right side. Copy?"

"Roger, Daze. Don't get shot by these idiots."

"Ditto," she said, and slipped down the uphill side of the tree.

"Looks like a squad," Cutty said. "Nothing we can't handle."

"Copy," she said, and creeped to the right, under cover of the trees on the hillside.

The Germans reached the front door and pounded on it.

Lagunas found a spot and crouched there. She trained her M4A1 on the men standing on the front porch.

The lights in the house went out.

Good.

She looked at the men on the porch.

Are they dumb? Why aren't they flanking the house?

She turned to her right. There was movement where the hedge met the hillside. She switched her goggles to thermal imaging. Several men were creeping around the hedge.

In moments, her position would be indefensible. Shortly after that, the general would be taken. Or killed.

Lagunas slipped off her goggles. She moved behind a tree, rose with her back to it, and took a deep breath.

She slipped from behind the tree and shot the first two men in the creeping squad. She spun to her left and shot a man on the porch, then took off uphill. The squad returned fire at her earlier position. The men from the porch scurried to cover behind the hedge. Under cover of the trees, she ran to the refuge of the oaks.

"What was that, Daze?" Cutty said.

"There's another squad flanking the house from the right."

"Copy," he said. "I'll call for help."

Lagunas heard Cutty whisper again. "More people are over at the bridge. Looks like platoon strength. We're screwed unless we get backup. Why don't you get the general and Will Lee up and out the back windows?"

"Roger," she said.

Lagunas peeked around the corner of the house to check on the Germans coming from the right flank. They were moving again, but much more cautiously.

She dashed back across the width of the house and slipped through the window to Washington's bedroom. He wasn't there. She checked the other back bedroom for Lee, but he wasn't there either.

They must be downstairs.

She descended the stairs as quietly as she could.

The Joyner family stood near the front door. Able, Mattie, and the oldest boy had muskets at the ready. Washington stood with them, with sword and pistol in hand. Lee, ever protective of his master, held a musket and stood between him and the door.

"General Washington," she whispered.

Everyone spun around to train their weapons on her. Mattie Joyner let out a gasp.

Daze dropped her weapon and it swung down by her side, restrained by its strap. She held up her hands.

"I'm a friend."

"She is our friend," Washington said. "I told you about them. She and Lieutenant Cutty have been following me all evening for protection."

"Sorry to surprise you," Lagunas said. "General, we must get you out of here. Come this way — we'll slip out the upstairs window and escape uphill."

"Sorry, Lieutenant," Washington said, "but I'll not leave my friends here to fight these people by themselves."

Daze looked at the children.

"We can't defeat them or survive a battle with them," she said, then turned to Washington again. "They have automatic rifles, like the one we showed you yesterday. There are forty soldiers out there."

"But we have a decent position here," Able said. "Better than in the woods at night with children."

Washington nodded at Lagunas and turned to his friend.

"Able, she's right. We can't defend against their strength. We have to retreat. Is there someplace you can go?"

"Yes," Mattie said. "The Youngs live on the other side of the mountain. They'll take us in. But it's not us they want, is it?"

"That's right," Daze said, "but they won't spare you if the general isn't here. I doubt they'll try to track you down if you leave his company, but right now, we just need to get you all out of here."

Able hesitated, then nodded. "If you say so, General. What do you need us to do?"

Lagunas knelt in front of the children.

"What are your names?"

Each child answered.

"Good," she said. "My name is Daisy. Can you all be brave and help me get your momma and your daddy away from these bad men?"

The children nodded.

"I knew I could count on you," she said, and rose.

Able knelt before the children. He gathered them in his arms and told them to obey every command from Daisy without talking.

The children hugged their father and ascended the stairs. Able stood.

"They know what to do," he said. "We drilled them on what to do if there's an Indian attack."

Lagunas nodded and ushered everyone upstairs and out the back window.

Cutty was on the ground, waiting for them. He inclined his head toward the barn.

"Help is on the way," he said. "I threw my beacon over there so Hatcher has a target for her jump. We gotta go — the place is crawling with unfriendlies. You guys start uphill, and I'll wait for Hatcher."

A brilliant light behind the barn drew their attention.

"There she is," he said. "Go! I'll collect her and join you."

****

Wednesday, February 11th, 2037 - 2:31 AM EST - HERO Team Lab, Telegraph Road, Alexandria, Virginia

The duty phone woke Hatcher from her sleep on the break room table. She jumped to her feet and studied it.

<Cutty: Facing a platoon of German soldiers. Need back up or we're screwed. Pls ACK. >

"Oh, crap," she said under her breath. She typed in a response.

<Hatcher: On my way, more to follow. Coordinates? >

While she waited, she forwarded Cutty's text to McKnight, then to Smalls and Tyler.

<Cutty: Land on my beacon. Bring me another. Landing zone is clear. >

Good God!

Hatcher typed in a final message.

<Hatcher: Wilco. Save some for me. >

She dashed to the console, looked up Cutty's beacon number, and captured its location. She duplicated the beacon and set the jump coordinates to take her there.

The duty phone rang. It was McKnight.

"Colonel, it's Hatcher here."

"I saw the message. What's happening?"

"I'm programming the Engine to take me there. I forwarded the message to Major Smalls and Major Tyler, but I'm going ahead. They need help now."

"Understood," McKnight said. "We'll join you as soon as we can. It may be thirty minutes. So go ahead. Where's Wheeler?"

"I don't know, sir. I—"

The lab doors flew open, and Wheeler charged into the room.

"Oh, he's here, sir."

"Good, take him along. Make us proud."

"Yes, sir," she said, and disconnected the call.

Wheeler stood before her, his hands on his hips. "You weren't thinking of going without me, were you?"

"What? Are you sleeping here now?"

"Just tonight. Thought you might want my help," he said.

"Okay, I've set a five second delay on the trigger so we can send ourselves off."

"Roger," he said. "Race you to the weapons locker." He was moving before the words left his lips.

"Asshole," she said, and chased him to the locker. They pulled out cold-weather gear, a pair of M4A1s, body armor, and extra ammo clips.

Wheeler swung an M60 machine gun over his shoulder and grabbed an ammo box.

"Are you gonna carry all that?" Hatcher asked.

"Better to have it and not need it," he said. "Besides, it's Cutty's favorite gun and he can carry it when we get there."

He trailed behind her with his equipment load as they hurried back to the platform.

Hatcher ran to the console and checked the coordinates once more. Then she pressed the trigger and joined Wheeler on the platform. They gathered their gear in their arms to be sure everything made the jump.

The pale blue aura surrounded them.

Hatcher looked at Wheeler, and he grinned back at her.

"I've always wanted to fight against Nazis," he said.

Then she saw nothing but the stars of time travel.

CHAPTER SEVENTEEN

Tuesday, February 11th, 1787 - 2:38 AM EST - Able and Mattie Joyner's Farm, The Woods of Northern Virginia

Hatcher and Wheeler landed in 1787.

At first, it was too dark to see. After the brilliance of the travel aura, their eyes needed to adjust to the scant light of a Virginia valley at night.

Hatcher frowned.

Damn! I hate to jump into a combat zone with no vision.

As they slowly regained their night vision, the sound of rifle fire echoed around the buildings.

They were boxed into a grassy yard, bordered by a barn on their left, a forested hill on their right, and a two-story house fifteen yards in front of them.

First order of business. Night vision goggles.

"Did all your stuff make it here?" she asked.

Wheeler looked up from his weapons. "It did. Where the hell are we?"

"On a farm. Cutty said he was sending us to a clear landing zone."

A machine gun rattled nearby. They both tensed and brought their weapons forward in response. The gun was too far away to be aimed at them, but close enough to get their attention. The sound of bullets striking the ground and trees uphill told them where the gun was shooting.

Good luck hitting anything up there.

She drew in a quick breath.

That's where our people are.

They crept along the side of the barn to the corner nearest the house and peeped around it. There were men coming at the front of the house from behind a hedge, and there was a machine gun in the hedge, firing up into the trees.

They pulled back from the building's corner.

"How many?" Hatcher whispered.

"I count six, plus the machine gun."

"Ditto. Okay. Let's even the odds, shall we? I'll fire a dozen rounds at the riflemen and you take Cutty's gun and pound away at that machine gun position. At minimum, they'll have to move the gun and advance more slowly."

"Roger. Let me get Cutty's M60."

"Wait," she said, and pointed. "Look! There's Cutty, behind the farmhouse."

Cutty slid down the hillside by the house and sprinted across the open space toward them.

The machine gunner saw Cutty and tried to get his gun out in front to lead him, but the best he could manage was to stitch bullets across the yard behind him.

Several of the riflemen fired at him and two bullets struck him in the back. He fell, but his momentum carried him behind the barn. He sprawled on his face and didn't move.

"Dammit," Hatcher yelled, and fired at the riflemen as they advanced, wounding three before they retreated to the hedge.

The machine gun stopped firing, and she knew why.

He's turning to shoot at me.

Wheeler pulled her back and fired the M60 at the gunner's position. He turned the section of hedge around the gun into a shower of leaves as his bullets crashed through it. The machine gun in the hedge fired a burst of ten rounds, then fell silent. Wheeler fired for a few more seconds, then looked back at Cutty. Hatcher was kneeling by him.

She pushed hard to roll the big man over onto his back. He looked up at her.

"Damn, that hurt," he said. "I hate those people."

Wheeler joined her at Cutty's side.

"Thank God for body armor," she said. "Can you get up? Are you okay?"

Cutty's eyes closed, and he said, "Is that you, Ma? Carry me, please?"

Hatcher punched him in the solar plexus.

"Get up, asshole," she said. "He's fine, Wheeler."

"Roger that."

Cutty sat up, rubbing his solar plexus.

"Hey, I brought you a present," Wheeler said. He handed Cutty the M60 and pointed at the barn's wall. "The ammo box is over there. Get loaded up."

Cutty ran his hands over the weapon and grinned. "Now, that's what I'm talking about."

"You'll like this, too," Wheeler said, and handed him his new return beacon.

"Ah, thanks."

"Where's the general and Daze?" Hatcher asked.

"They're uphill about half a klick," Cutty said. "We need to get up there fast. There's another squad on the other side of the house, shooting up in the woods. Any time now, they're going to realize the general is escaping and head up that way. By herself, Daze will have her hands full."

"How many have y'all killed?" she said.

"I've killed a couple. Daze did, too. We just tried to keep them at bay. There's too many to assault."

"We've put down six or seven," she said. "Let's do more damage before we go. They'll get adventurous again in a few minutes."

"What do you want to do?" Wheeler asked.

"Give 'em a bloody nose and make 'em think we're more than squad size, right?" She looked up at the barn's second story.

It's tall enough.

"Does this barn have a loft? We need some high ground."

"Yes, it does."

"Awesome. Okay, Wheeler? Scout around to the opposite barn corner, the one that's diagonal from this one." She patted the wall next to her. "Cutty, you take up position here with the M60."

"Roger," Cutty said.

"Where are you going?" Wheeler asked.

"The loft. Wait until I'm in position if you can. Start firing when I do. As soon as they turn back for cover, fire two more bursts and high-tail it up the hill. Got it?"

"Damn straight," Wheeler said. "See you on the other side."

Hatcher touched her carbine's barrel to his. "Give 'em hell."

She patted Wheeler's shoulder as he stood and swept past her. Cutty moved to the near corner, and she ran after Wheeler to the barn's back side. He passed the barn's back door and stopped at the far corner.

Hatcher stepped through the back door, swinging her weapon right and left. She found the ladder to the loft and climbed it. It was pitch black, but her goggles made it easy to find the loft door that faced the house. She crawled to it, eased the door open a crack, and peeked through it.

The yard was full of soldiers creeping forward.

Maybe fifteen.

She opened fire. As the Germans looked up at her position, Cutty's M60 began firing.

Before the troopers realized they were in trouble and retreated, they lost three more men.

Hatcher left her position and half-fell, half-climbed from the loft. She sprinted for the door. Outside, Cutty's M60 hammered twice more and went silent. She heard bullets stitching across the wall to her right.

They flanked us!

At the door, she saw muzzle flashes in the woods behind them. She dropped to the ground and brought her weapon forward to shoot. From her right, Wheeler's M4A1 rattled as he fired at the flashes.

The gun in the woods stopped shooting.

Wheeler ran to her, grabbed her wrist, and pulled her to her feet. "For Christ's sake, Hatcher, let's get the hell out of here."

The two sprinted for the safety of the forest behind the house. Ahead, she saw Cutty disappear into the woods and up the hillside.

Good!

As they reached the trees, grenades clattered on the barn's floor. They were ten meters uphill before an explosion shivered the building and set it on fire.

As they ran up the slope, Wheeler spoke between labored breaths. "How the hell did that guy get behind us?"

"I don't know," she said. "Maybe he was a scout who didn't get back before the shooting started."

They caught up to Cutty thirty meters up the hillside.

"Cutty, where's the General and Daze?"

"Straight up the hill," he said.

"Okay," Wheeler said. "We need to find them. Cutty, take the lead."

The three officers set a brutal pace.

After fifty meters, they heard a half-whispered challenge.

"Siberian!"

They stopped in their tracks. Wheeler grinned at Hatcher and called out, "Khatru."

"Pass, friend," the voice responded.

Ten more steps brought them face-to-face with Daze, General Washington, and Will Lee.

"Man, am I glad to see you guys," Daze said. "It was getting pretty lonely up here in the woods in the dark."

Hatcher noticed the Joyners standing close behind Washington.

"Are these your friends you were staying with?"

"Look!" Will Lee said, and pointed downhill. The barn and the farmhouse were burning.

"Did you say these people are Hessians from the future?" Washington asked.

"Pretty much, sir," Daze said.

"It appears their tactics haven't changed much." He turned to the Joyners. "Able, I'm sorry I brought this on you. I didn't expect them to follow me. I did not understand the risk. If I had, I never would have brought this disaster upon you."

Joyner stared at the raging fires that were their house and barn. Mattie clutched his arm and whispered, "Our home." Tears rolled down her cheeks.

"Get hold of yourself, Mattie," Able said. "Now look around you. We're still alive and we can rebuild. What's happened here is important."

Mattie sniffled and wiped the tears from her eyes. "You're right, of course," she said. "Let's get the children and ourselves to safety."

She gathered the kids and retreated a few yards up the hill.

Joyner turned back to Washington. "What's the plan, General?"

"For you?" the General asked. "Keep your family safe. What next, Captain… Hatcher, isn't it?"

"Yes, sir," Hatcher said. "Here's what I suggest, General. They won't stop. Chances are good they're already doing a recon up this way. Lieutenant Lagunas picked a suitable spot here. She will escort you, Will, and the Joyners further back up the hill. Cutty, Wheeler, and I will set up an ambush here."

Washington shook his head. "Under no circumstances will I leave you and your people to fight and perhaps die on my account. I'm standing here with you. Give me a weapon."

"I'm not leaving either," Will said. "I go where General Washington goes. I'm his man. and I still have my Brown Bess."

Hatcher looked at the two men.

One black, the other white. One a slave, the other a landowner and a general. Both were unwilling to retreat while others faced mortal danger on their behalf.

"Cutty, give me your M4," she said. "You have the M60."

Cutty unslung the weapon from his shoulder and handed it to her. She passed it to Washington and pointed to the carbine in his arms.

"It kicks a little, but nothing like your Brown Bess. See where it says safe-semi-auto? That's a safety mechanism. Move the switch from safe to auto and it will fire as long as you pull the trigger until you run out. You have thirty bullets. By the time you shoot them all, we'll be on our way out of here. Here's the strategy. They come up the hill, we shoot a few of them, then retreat while they're trying to figure out if we're still here or gone. Got it?"

Washington grinned.

Hatcher was stunned. She had never seen him smile. As far as she knew, there were no paintings of Washington with a smile on his face.

"I understand the strategy," he said. "I used it against the British for seven years."

"Of course you did," she said, and blushed. *What was I thinking?*

"Daze?" she said. "Gather the Joyners and move out. Gentlemen, let's prepare to kill the enemy."

Washington and the HERO officers piled dead wood on the downhill side of their position. Then they laid behind it and watched the downhill woods. "Fire when I do," Hatcher whispered.

The enemy was not long in coming.

She peered into the dark with her goggles. She could see movement thirty meters away.

"Here they come," she whispered. "Looks like about twenty-five of them. Wait for me to fire, then let 'em have it."

She looked at Washington, and he nodded back to her.

That old guy's got balls of steel, even with all this new stuff thrown at him.

The Germans were less than ten meters away when Hatcher opened fire.

Three fell dead at once. Two more fell as they retreated.

We've got three minutes before they regroup and try to flank us.

She turned to the others.

"Go!" she said and dashed to Cutty as the others fled uphill.

"When they lift their heads, fire a few bursts. Hit 'em if you can. When they go back down, haul ass after us."

"Yes, ma'am."

Hatcher sprinted after the others.

She caught them as the M60 fired again.

She glanced back.

C'mon, Cutty!

After climbing another thirty meters, they heard another burst from the M60.

Before them was a well-traveled road.

They stood for a moment.

Hatcher shrugged and whispered, "Which way did they go?"

"Beats me," Wheeler said.

They whirled at sounds behind them. It was Cutty, breathing hard.

"I think I need a few more hours of PT," he said.

"Shhh," Hatcher said. "I hear something."

A soft voice said, "Siberian."

"Khatru!" Wheeler said.

"Pass, friend."

Daze stepped out of the darkness in front of them.

Washington stepped forward. "Where are the Joyners?"

"They're gone. They have friends about two miles down this road, and they wanted to go before the fighting got worse."

"Can't say I blame them," Wheeler said. "The Germans would have killed them if they caught them with us, but I'm sure they have no interest in pursuing them."

"I am comforted," Washington said. "I would hate for them to suffer any more for my sake."

"Listen," Cutty said, and pointed downhill.

They heard men tramping through the woods.

"What do you think?" Hatcher asked Wheeler.

He listened for a moment. "There were more than we thought. There's at least twenty-five coming after us. We have the high ground, but against those numbers… It doesn't look good."

"What are our options?" Washington said.

"Fight and get away," Wheeler said.

"Or die," Hatcher said. She looked at Washington and shrugged. "I know you want the truth."

"Thank you," Washington said. "Shall we hit them again?"

"From your words to God's ears," Wheeler said, and looked at the sky. "You heard that, right? I know the general is one of your favorites, so we're counting on you."

"I did a little recon while waiting for you guys," Daze said. "I know a place. There's a shelf in the mountainside about thirty meters further up. It's got decent cover and a good view of this road."

"Show me, Daze," Hatcher said.

They followed her to the shelf.

"Not bad if we had more people," Wheeler said. "It's exposed on the flanks, but it has a solid front. This will work for a little while."

"Yes, sir," Daze said. She turned to Hatcher. "I'll go get the others."

"Good," Hatcher said. She and Wheeler stood in silence for a moment.

"It's better than anywhere else up here," she said. "But if they flank us here on one side, we're in trouble. If they flank us on two sides—"

"We're dead. I know."

"And we've got to assume they know what they're doing."

Washington and the others reached the shelf. He looked around, then approached them.

"Pardon me for interrupting, Major, but I suspect you're thinking of what happens when they flank us. Am I correct?"

"Yes, sir," Hatcher said. "This place will suffice for an ambush and quick retreat, but then where do we go? We're dead if they flank us on both sides."

"I agree," Washington said. "What are our options?"

"Hey, I'm getting a message from the lab," Cutty said. "The Colonel, Smalls, and Tyler are ready to join us. How do I respond?"

Washington held up his hand. "What if they *do* join us?"

Hatcher nodded ascent. "Cutty, tell them to stand by a minute."

She looked at Washington. "They add significant firepower and smarts. No doubt they will improve our situation."

"Damn straight!" Wheeler said.

"But... we'll still be in an untenable position," she said. "Seven from our team, plus you and Will. Against twenty-five or more. We'll still be out-manned and out-gunned. We'll kill a lot of them, but we'll take casualties. As soon as they get close enough, they'll start tossing grenades up here. We have no defense against that. If we get away, we'll still be on the run. Do you agree, Wheeler?"

Wheeler pulled at his lower lip. "I do. We could still run, but there'll be no stopping. They'll run us down, eventually."

"You're leaving out the obvious option, aren't you?" Washington asked.

"What option, sir?"

"What do you call it... a time jump? Can they follow us to your time?"

"I haven't mentioned it, because it's your call, sir. But now that you've brought it up... It's the best option. We all escape. They can't follow us. But you'll be in the distant future... a place you were reluctant to go."

Washington shrugged. "I think I *do* prefer it to death." He turned around and called Will to him.

"Will, do you prefer death or a jump with these people to their time?"

"General Washington, I go where you go."

"I understand, Will, but I know nothing about this future. I can't expect you to come along when —"

"Excuse me, sir," Will said. "Begging your pardon, sir, but I've followed you all over these colonies during the war. And I don't want to die here. Where else would I go?"

"Where else, indeed. Of course, you must come along."

"So it is," he said to Hatcher. "Well, Captain? Do we have a consensus?"

A burst of machine gun fire from the woods below the road caused them to duck. The rounds ricocheted off the rocks above their heads.

"Shall we return fire, Captain?" Cutty said.

Hatcher shook her head. "Not yet, Lieutenant. Let's huddle."

Cutty and Daze walked over to them.

"We're jumping out," Hatcher said. "Cutty, send a status to the Console. Tell them not to come. We're jumping home with the General and Will Lee ASAP."

"Roger, ma'am," Cutty said, then tapped out the message response.

"Okay, here's how we'll do it," Wheeler said. "Daze, you take the General with you. Hatcher will take Will with her. Cutty and I will remain to provide covering fire, then jump out together after the rest of you are safe. Clear?"

"Yes, sir," each of them said.

"Okay, here's the order of operation. By priority and thirty seconds apart, Daze and the General will go first. Then Hatcher and Will Lee, then me and Cutty."

"No," Washington said. "Will and Lieutenant Hatcher go first. If I go first and anything happens to him... I don't want that on my conscience."

Hatcher shook her head. "You understand our priorities, sir, right? You must go first." She stood before him with her feet spread apart and her arms crossed.

"No, Captain Hatcher," Washington said. "Will goes first. On this, I must stand firm."

Another machine gun burst stitched its way across the rocky face above and behind them.

Hatcher shook her head, then nodded. "You're the general, sir. Will and I will go first, and you must follow us."

"We will, Captain. I have no desire to be shot."

Hatcher pulled Will away from the others and into a kneeling position with her.

"This keeps us from falling backward when we get there." She double-clicked her beacon.

The travel aura formed around them.

As they fell into the stars of time travel, she chuckled to herself.

Who knew? Here I am, jumping through time with George Washington's butler in my arms.

The End of Episode One – Hail Mary Pass

The Story continues in Episode Two – Stranger
(Available August 15th, 2023)

<u>A Note from the Author</u>

Thanks for reading this book.

For a short note from me, please scan the QR code below.

Cheers and regards,
Kim

Books by Kim Megahee

The Marc McKnight Time Travel Adventures

Book 1 – TIME LIMITS

Book 2 – THE TIME TWISTERS

Book 3 – TIME REVOLUTION

Book 4 – TIME PLAGUE

The Time Patriot Series

Episode 1 – HAIL MARY PASS

Episode 2 – STRANGER

Episode 3 – POLITICS

Episode 4 – SURVIVAL

About the Author

Kim Megahee is a writer, musician, and retired computer consultant. He has a degree from the University of Georgia in Mathematics Education. His background includes playing in rock bands, teaching high school, and much experience in computer programming, security, and consulting.

In addition to writing, he enjoys hanging out with his wife, reading, boating on Lake Lanier, playing live music, promoting literature, and socializing with friends. Kim lives in Gainesville, Georgia with his soulmate wife Martha and Leo, the brilliant and stubborn red-headed toy poodle.

www.AuthorKimMegahee.com

Facebook: author.kmega

The Northeast Georgia Literary Society:

www.NEGALiterarySociety.com

www.ingramcontent.com/pod-product-compliance
Lightning Source LLC
Chambersburg PA
CBHW071346170626
46811CB00003B/1010